CRAIG MARTELLE

MICHAEL ANDERLE

NOMAD AVENGED

A KUTHERIAN GAMBIT SERIES
TERRY HENRY WALTON CHRONICLES
BOOK 7

*They say behind every great man, is a great woman,
but what if the woman is a Werewolf?*

COPYRIGHT

DEDICATION

We can't write without those who support us
On the home front, we thank you for being there for us

We wouldn't be able to do this for a living if it weren't for our readers
We thank you for reading our books

Nomad Avenged
The Terry Henry Walton Chronicles
Team Includes

BETA / EDITOR BOOK
Leo Roars, Diane Velasquez, & Dorene Johnson – they read this in the
draft stage and caught enough that made us do a complete rewrite.

JIT Beta Readers - From both of us, our deepest gratitude!

John Raisor
James Caplan
Micky Cocker
Kimberly Boyer
Alex Wilson
Joshua Ahles
Kelly ODonnell
Ginger Sparkman
Micky Cocker
Thomas Ogden
John Findlay
Paul Westman
Sherry Foster
Keith Verret
Mike Pendergrass

*If I missed anyone, **please** let me know!*

TIMELINE

World's Worst Day Ever (WWDE)
WWDE+20 years – Terry Henry Walton Returns to humanity
    Nomad Found
    Nomad Redeemed
    Nomad Unleashed
WWDE+23 years – Terry & Char get married in New Boulder
    Nomad Supreme
WWDE+24 years – The move to North Chicago is complete,
Kaeden & Kimber join Terry & Char's family
    Nomad's Fury
WWDE+25 years – Cordelia is born
    Nomad's Justice
WWDE+50 years – Terry Henry is taken prisoner
    Nomad Avenged
WWDE+50-100 years – Nomad Mortis
WWDE+125 years – Nomad's Force
WWDE+145 years – Nomad's Galaxy

PROLOGUE

ONE MONTH BEFORE THE WWDE...

Gilbert Kirkus had never been the strongest, but usually was the brightest. Addicted to knowledge, his face was always in a book. Along with being gifted, he studied hard. Columbia for his undergrad and MIT for his PhD. He had no equal in his class.

Everyone had been bigger and stronger than Kirkus, but he refused to be intimidated by size.

Kirkus had become one of the top engineers with a defense contractor. His ambition started to outweigh his thirst for knowledge. He didn't understand why he hadn't been vaulted into the CEO's corner office. Kirkus learned what it was like to hate.

One evening, the company met with a group of strange people who had a different air about them. The leadership of Kirkus's firm seemed to be afraid of this group. Kirkus had simply been curious. He was invited as the senior engineer, despite his newfound abrasiveness, because the group had some interesting proposals and a short timeline for implementation.

The group, headed by Mister Smith, would only meet at night. Kirkus didn't believe that was the pasty-looking man's real name, but he had the appropriate clearance, which meant that he'd been vetted.

Kirkus didn't care about any of that. He was fascinated by their claims of working with certain technologies, like nanites that worked within the bloodstream and anti-gravity for propulsion. Kirkus was taken by both.

Mr. Smith's small entourage showed some of the math and discussed just enough of the engineering to convince Kirkus. No one else understood. The contractor's leadership considered the information to be theoretical and were dismissive. They remained fearful. Kirkus could see it in their eyes. They only wanted the group to go away.

Not Kirkus. He believed, and he was smitten.

When the meeting wrapped up at midnight, the group invited Kirkus to join them at a downtown club. Although he'd never been interested in Washington D.C.'s nightlife, he didn't want to miss an opportunity to question them further about the math and science.

He almost forgot his ambitions when these new challenges appeared.

That night, he learned Mr. Smith's true nature. That night, he learned the most important lesson of his life—that he could never go back.

❖ ❖ ❖

Kirkus woke in a strange bed, in a strange room.

The change.

The nanocytes coursing through his body. He could feel what they were doing to him.

Or was it only in his mind?

Kirkus gripped the edge of the bed as his mind and his body wrestled for control.

Jekyll and Hyde. Bela Lugosi as Dracula. Visions raced through his mind on a river of pain.

The hunger. His stomach twisted in knots. It wanted what it wanted, nothing that he'd ever tasted before but had to have.

He tore from the room, singularly focused on one thing. No one was there.

Kirkus was all alone. But there were sounds, noises from outside.

He yanked the door open to a fading sunset. The brightness of the setting sun slammed into him like a shockwave.

He was thrown back and landed heavily. Kirkus crawled to a dark corner, out of the light and away from the pain as he nursed the burns on his tender skin. He passed out.

When he woke up, it was the middle of night, dark outside. Hands were fumbling through his clothes. The man jumped back when he saw the glowing red eyes.

"Whoa, buddy, sorry. We thought you was homeless just like us. You know how it is. Nothing personal, friend. We'll leave you be," the other man said as he finished going through Kirkus's pockets.

Kirkus grabbed the man by the throat in a crushing grip. He stood and lifted the stranger until his feet dangled above the ground. The first man tried to run. Kirkus kicked his feet. The man stumbled and fell. Kirkus held him down with his foot.

The hunger, it pulled him in. He knew what to do without ever having done it before.

His body knew.

Kirkus's canines extended, hollowed, and he bit deeply into the man's neck, finding the carotid.

Nourishment. So much more than eating.

Kirkus threw the shriveled corpse to the side as his body reveled in the strength surging through his veins. There was more he could eat, but not yet. His mind came back to him, seeking to regain control.

"Not yet, my friend, but I have plans for you," Kirkus told the terrified man squirming underfoot.

Kirkus picked him up, punched him a few times to settle him, and carried the man upstairs where he locked him inside the room in which Kirkus had earlier found himself.

He had found a new him. The pain had unleashed something incredible.

❖ ❖ ❖

Kirkus only saw Mr. Smith one more time, on the night before the WWDE. As a fellow Vampire, Kirkus was one of the newcomers, subordinate to Mr. Smith, who had shared his nanocytes and allowed Kirkus to change, become one of the elite.

One of the Forsaken, as others called them.

"What do you think of our ride?" Mr. Smith asked from within the small hangar on the outskirts of a rural Virginia town.

"Not very aerodynamic," were the first words out of Kirkus's mouth.

"Stop thinking like a Neanderthal," Mr. Smith had

cautioned. "What if air resistance was eliminated by creating a bubble around the ship, by accelerating by way of anti-gravity device using standard Newtonian physics?"

"It's not theory?" Kirkus asked. Mr. Smith backhanded Kirkus across the face.

"I thought you were supposed to be smart. We don't have time for me to paint a picture for you. Accept what you see and we can continue." The Vampire looked down at him. Kirkus was appropriately chastened, while at the same time invigorated. He was being intellectually challenged. His body had become something incredible.

And his mind. He found that he heard wisps from other people's minds. He erected walls to stop the bombardment of nonsense. He didn't want to be bothered by their limited understanding of the universe. Mr. Smith was a telepath, a rarity in the Unknown World, of which Kirkus had only recently been made a member.

"Exactly," Mr. Smith said aloud. "We can't be bothered by the trivial. Rise above it all, my son. Know that we are higher on the food chain. Normal humans are beneath us. Now and for all time, they will be beneath us. They are beasts of burden, tools, and food. Nothing more."

Kirkus nodded his agreement. He could see the wisdom in it all. The pain was gone. He'd survived his rite of passage, while reducing the homeless population of D.C.

They were food. Nothing more.

"The Sacred Clan Weretigers brought us this gift, a pod that they claim they stole from Bethany Anne's people." Mr. Smith made a face, "We believe it is technology from New Schwabenland, but either way, it is more advanced than anything with regular propulsion."

When the world collapsed, Kirkus was still in the remote

town studying the pod, as they called it. He'd been assigned a watcher from the Sacred Clan itself, a beautiful Chinese woman named Yanmei.

Vampires, Weretigers, and technology so advanced that only science fiction had dreamed of it.

Kirkus found that he didn't care if humanity survived or not. He waited a couple weeks, dining regularly on looters who stopped by the hangar. It was convenient that food came to him, almost like room service. He laughed as he gained strength.

Yanmei started training him how to fight. He'd never had to before and figured that he would be able to overcome any enemy, simply because of the power within.

The Weretiger told him that a time would come when that wouldn't be enough. He'd have to fight and fight well.

She remained distant. He expected they'd become lovers. He learned quickly that that wouldn't be the case, and would never be the case. She kicked his ass so hard, it made him question who was higher on the food chain. She liked it that way, but he improved quickly until he could stand his own against her.

In no time, he discovered that he was faster and stronger. Vampires.

The top of the food chain.

CHAPTER ONE

The room was darkened. It was meant to be, as most prisons were. Kirkus had gone to great lengths to prepare this room for this very purpose.

Great lengths and great sacrifice, but the Forsaken's trophy was there, hanging in the chains. Kirkus was both triumphant and furious.

Terry Henry Walton winced in pain and gasped for air. His nanocytes fought to keep up with the damage done to his body, but they were losing the battle.

The chains cut into his wrists; blood dripped slowly down his arms. One shoulder was dislocated. He'd hung there too long, feet barely touching the ground, unable to support himself when he passed out.

The Forsaken looked at his prisoner, pleased that the feeding marks still shown waxy red, but that didn't outweigh his anger. He was furious that Terry's nanocytes had killed one of his minions.

The *bite* that killed.

Kirkus considered himself a genius for not attempting the first feeding on the enhanced Terry Henry Walton. That he made a *minion* do it.

The Forsaken had yet to ask Terry any questions. He didn't need to. At the moment, Terry passed out and the instant when he returned to consciousness, he was vulnerable and Kirkus exploited that. Even with the anguish of being in chains, Terry maintained enough mental discipline to hold back most of the Vampire's probes.

Once Kirkus was inside Terry's incredible mind, he explored much that the human thought about, his enhancements at Bethany Anne's hand, his exploits with the FDG, and his work with Akio.

Especially his work with Akio.

Kirkus had seen TH's moral compass, and it made his Forsaken hair stand on end. Kirkus had never met an individual like Terry Henry Walton. A *pure soul,* some would call him. A person who knew Forsaken and didn't hate them. He considered them people who deserved a chance to prove themselves.

He saw the colonel joking with the one called Joseph. A Forsaken and the human, having a laugh. Kirkus made a fist and drove it into TH's ribs. The colonel grunted as his head lolled on his sweaty chest.

Terry's tongue felt like a dry rag stuffed in his mouth. The air didn't come quickly enough, and he stopped fighting it, letting himself slip into the darkness.

And Kirkus dove back in at that moment of weakness.

❖ ❖ ❖

NORTH CHICAGO

Char's eyes locked on Timmons's, the purple flaring. Without warning, her fist lashed out, shattering his eye socket and sending him sprawling. She growled, more animal than human.

"If you fucking limp dicks had done your job, Terry wouldn't have been captured. HOW IN THE FUCK DID YOU LET THAT HAPPEN?" she screamed, spittle flying from her mouth. The pack had failed her, had failed the entire community.

She viciously kicked a withering body.

"Look at this shit! He fought this fucking army by himself," she snarled. Eight Forsaken lay dead, shredded by whip and knife. TH had not gone easily. No whining, no running. He had fought, toe-to-toe, but in the end, there had been too many. She studied the marks on the ground. At least four of them had carried Terry into their ship.

"We heard it take off, but we didn't hear it land. How?" she wondered, but none of the pack knew.

"Cory?" Char asked her daughter.

Cordelia had grown into a near twin of her mother over the past twenty-five years.

Time had been kind to them both. The only difference between them was in their eyes and the faint scar that trailed to the edge of Char's mouth from the fight with her former mate decades earlier.

Cory's twenty-six-year-old body was lean and hard. She carried herself confidently and spoke intelligently. Her blue eyes sparkled, just like her father's. Her hair was almost like her mother's. She had the silver streak down the side, except Cory's hair was black. Her mark of the Werewolf was her furry wolf ears.

She considered that her cross to bear, especially since she wasn't a Werewolf.

It wasn't a very heavy cross, though, and she wore her hair long, to keep her ears covered as much as possible.

"It is Dad's blood, but not a terrible amount. He was unconscious when they carried him away. For whatever reason, I know in my heart and soul that he is still alive. We must move quickly, overwhelm them as they overwhelmed him. Is Akio on his way?" Cory asked.

"Soon. He told us yesterday that he would have to deal with a small Forsaken infestation in China. It cannot have been a coincidence. I don't care why, except in how that will help us know where he is. Then we go get him as soon as possible. All of us." Her last statement was aimed at the pack--Timmons, Ted, Adams, Merritt, Shonna, and Sue. She also included the Weretiger Aaron and the Werebear Gene in her piercing gaze.

No one disputed her. She was the alpha, and her mate had been taken.

The sun was just starting to rise. The ship that had carried Terry away should not have existed. It had been almost fifty years since the fall, the World's Worst Day Ever, and industry was starting to make a comeback, but not enough to build airplanes.

"Maybe it was a pod or some alien craft. Have they returned to Earth? Has Bethany Anne lost the battle and we're being invaded?" Char wondered, looking helplessly at the tracks on the ground and where the aircraft's landing struts had crushed the grass.

"No," Timmons ventured. Terry Henry Walton left all the evidence behind that they needed. "It was a Forsaken who has been rebuilding, just like we're doing here, but he's flown under our radar. Now we know he's there, and we'll make him pay."

Timmons rubbed his crushed eye socket as his nanocytes knitted the bone together, rebuilding his face. The pain was mostly gone. He didn't want another beating. He only wanted what was best for the pack, and that was to recover the alpha's mate.

"What do we tell the people?" Aaron asked softly.

Char looked at him out of the corner of her eye. She hadn't thought that far ahead.

❖ ❖ ❖

Time had not been kind to Billy Spires, but he was blessed in different ways. Marcie had grown up to be a lovely blond woman, short like her parents.

Billy and Felicity would have never guessed, on that first day when Terry Henry Walton walked into their lives, that their families would become inextricably linked and they would become lifelong friends.

Kaeden had grown up to be a hearty young man. Everyone was surprised that neither he nor Kimber joined the Force de Guerre. The FDG had its place, and although Kae and Kim often trained with them, they didn't deploy.

Their pasts made them appreciate family life so much that it physically pained them to be apart. When Marcie turned sixteen, Kae was in his early twenties. She blossomed, and he was smitten. They'd been friends forever, but she had always been a child.

Until she wasn't. All of a sudden, she became a woman, and Kaeden turned awkward. As soon as they started dating, he returned to being himself and they became inseparable. They waited before having children, but that was inevitable too, further cementing the family bond between Terry and Billy.

Billy leaned heavily on his cane. Marcie fussed over her toddler while Kaeden carried the baby. Felicity still looked young and vibrant. Like Char, she appeared to be a sister to her daughter, not her mother.

And she definitely did not look like a grandmother.

"Had I known that you received the gift of nanocytes, I wouldn't have changed anything," Billy said, his rough voice barely more than a croak. His hard life had caught up with him as he approached sixty-five years of age.

"I honestly never knew," Felicity drawled. "One day not long after the fall, I was hiding in the ruins. Someone came and I ran. I fell and was badly injured. When I woke up, I was different. Healed but different."

She shook her head as she thought back to that time. Afterward, she felt stronger and healed quickly whenever she was injured. That was when she headed for the hills, deciding to stay out of sight until she could find someone with enough power to make her comfortable.

She found New Boulder and Billy Spires. "When Terry showed up, I sensed that he had something similar to what I had, but so much greater. You know, Billy, I never wanted to be different like that. I wanted to be young and beautiful, but that was a stupid teenager's dream."

Felicity hugged her husband, holding him to keep from pushing the frail man down.

"This is the part that makes me question how worthwhile

it was. I'm going to lose you, Billy, and here I am, forced to live on without you. Marcie doesn't have the nanocytes, and neither do their kids. My greatest fear is that I'm going to outlive them all." Her blue eyes started to glisten. She blinked because she didn't want to cry. "Be careful what you ask for, because you may get it."

A tear trailed down Felicity's beautiful cheek. Her hair was styled, and she wore makeup like she always did. That was her persona, perpetually beautiful. She had always been the mayor's wife, it seemed, but no longer.

She was simply called the mayor now.

Without Billy, time was losing its luster. She thought about stepping down and moving on, but that wasn't what she wanted either. She liked being able to manage the town, take care of the people. Felicity wasn't going to get her greatest desire. She only wanted to grow old.

She laughed out loud.

"My, how times change, don't they, Billy dear?" she quipped, not expecting a response. He looked at her and smiled.

"I'll sit here and watch you play with the kids," he told her. They'd installed a bench outside the mayor's building a long time back. It was Billy and Felicity's favorite place. They watched the entire community pass through Mayor's Park at one point or another. It hosted all the best social gatherings of North Chicago.

Felicity patted Billy's arm and hurried down the steps into the park to join Kaeden and Marcie. For yet another in a seemingly infinite number of times, she walked on the grass of Mayor's Park.

This was their home and grass was their reward for moving from New Boulder to North Chicago. Terry Henry and

Charumati had made that happen, saved the people, saved the town.

Marcie had only been a toddler when they'd made the trip. Kaeden had joined the community during the move.

Kaeden had turned into a stout young man, barely taller than Billy, but wide and strong. He worked on the fishing boat most days, but not today. Six days on and one off. This happened to be his day to rest. He'd be back on the lake the next day.

Kaeden and Marcie's baby fussed in Kae's arms. "Do you need your mommy?" he asked little William, but Marcie gave him the stink-eye. He reconsidered his position, before adding, "No, you don't!"

He turned and walked away, bouncing the baby merrily and hoping to remain in the good graces of his beautiful wife. She smiled and shook her head at him.

"I love you," he mouthed to her. Terry had taught him that it was important to mean it and important to say it. He'd learned that late in life and didn't want Kae to miss out because he was a stubborn man.

"Just like his mother, that one," Felicity suggested. Marcie furled her brow.

"You're saying I was a fussy baby? That's not how I remember it," she retorted.

"People thought I was a mutant with a permanent attachment on my hip," Felicity replied, smiling. "You always needed to be bounced. If that's the worst of it? You're going to be just fine."

Marcie and Kae's daughter, the three-year-old Mary Ellen, ran away from her mother and grandmother, giggling. Felicity took chase and soon they found themselves on the other side of the park.

Kimber ran up, out of breath. "Where's Kae?" she demanded without explaining. The worry on her face surprised Felicity.

"What happened?" the mayor asked, turning to the side so Kim could see her brother.

"They've taken Father. The Forsaken have taken our father!"

Felicity didn't hesitate. She scooped up Mary Ellen and ran. Kim kept pace as they crossed the field. Kae stopped what he was doing, concern spreading across his face.

"Forsaken have taken Father. We need to join the FDG!" she insisted, waving William away when he reached toward his aunt. Her tone scared him, and he started to cry.

"I'm sorry, Liam," she cooed, but still wouldn't take him. Kae handed the boy to Marcie, kissing her on the cheek as he did so. He wrapped his fingers in his wife's blond hair and twirled one lock.

Her big blue eyes glistened, because she too was afraid. William started to cry harder as Marcie hugged him to her. "I'll come back to you. I'll always come home to you."

She nodded as her lips trembled. Kaeden couldn't stand to see her cry. It was heart-wrenching. He kissed her again and joined his sister as they ran for the FDG barracks.

❖ ❖ ❖

TERRY'S PRISON

"You are one sad fucker," Terry mumbled, blinking away the sweat and blood to better see his tormentor.

"Terry Henry Walton. You are renowned in many circles for your ability to sling a phrase, and the best you can come up with is 'sad fucker?' I am truly disappointed," Kirkus complained with a half-smile.

"My apologies to your sensibilities. Methink'st thou art a general offence and every man should beat thee," Terry quoted Shakespeare in a gravelly voice. "Or maybe, you are a gorbellied, fen-sucked coxcomb?"

Terry's mind was a jumble, but the mental exercise of stringing various Shakespearean words together to create insults comforted him. It reminded him of his daughter, named after one of Shakespeare's characters.

Cordelia. He saw the toddler in his mind's eye. He thought he heard something, but it faded into the distance. The only thing before him was his daughter.

She was barely walking, but fearless. Once she saved their lives after the wolverine attack, the wolf pack took to following her around. The former alpha walked at the child's side, letting her wrap her hand in the heavy neck hair to help her balance, help her run.

Terry looked away for only a moment. When he looked back, Cory was on the wolf's back, riding the bitch as nine others ran alongside. They disappeared into the woods on the south side of the former base that the people of North Chicago now called home.

He ran after them, jogging at first, but when he entered the woods, he couldn't hear the wolves at all. It was like they never passed through there, like they never existed.

Terry ran, as fast as his enhanced body would carry him, but he found no sign of the pack. He turned and ran home, needing to rally the people and search for his daughter.

When he entered Mayor's Park, he found Cory riding the wolf. They were running in circles.

"How'd you get back here?" he asked, wondering whether

it was a dream or a memory.

"We made a loop!" Cory said excitedly. The pack knew that she was a child and since they had adopted her, they were teaching her their ways, while also playing like a bunch of puppies. Terry Henry could not have been prouder.

Cory was growing up to know both the way of the pack and the way of humanity. As she matured, those lessons would keep her safe, but Terry always worried.

Terry's memory clouded for an instant, and when it cleared, it was more than a decade later.

Thirteen-year-old Cordelia was a beautiful young lady who looked too much like an adult. The men had too much to drink. Alcohol reduced one of them into a savage. He grabbed Cory by her hair and tried to kiss her.

Terry watched from a second-story window, unable to move. The young man needed to be taught a lesson, harshly enough that the young man would learn what civilization was all about.

What bothered Terry the most was that the man looked at Cory like a piece of meat and not an intelligent human being.

Cory kneed the man hard. Being tall like her parents, she was able to leverage more power into her move. The man came off the ground and crumpled, laying in the fetal position and crying. "BITCH!" the man yelled through gritted teeth.

Terry was angry and demanded retribution.

Cory kicked the man in the face, not a roundhouse but a snap-kick using a well-practiced technique. She laughed, musically, in a way that naturally drew others to her. She smiled, tossed her hair over her shoulders, and strolled away. Terry smiled.

Until someone slapped him.

"Come back to me, TH. I don't give a shit about your mutant spawn. Show me the woman with the purple eyes," Kirkus demanded, wiping Terry's sweat and blood from his hand with a rag.

"Love to, dickless, but shit-eating ass monkeys like you don't rate. Since we're talking about asses, why don't you go fuck yourself, Kirky-poo," Terry chuckled.

Kirkus snorted in derision and balled his fist, but he'd had enough of punching Terry Henry Walton. The man felt like he was made of steel. Kirkus wondered how a metal pipe would fare against a man of steel.

"I'll be right back, Mister Terry Henry Walton, and we can discuss purple eyes and all manner of things that I have in store for her," the Forsaken sneered.

Kirkus strolled away, dousing the light on his way out and plunging the room into complete darkness.

"That's Colonel, you asswipe."

CHAPTER TWO

NORTH CHICAGO

kio, answer, please answer," Char pleaded with the silent communication device. "Why won't you answer?" she bellowed, clenching her jaw, hands curling into fists.

She reared back to slam the device into the table but thought better of it. TH had the other device, and if they lost hers, then they would have no way of contacting Akio, guaranteeing that Terry Henry would be left alone to his fate.

She couldn't have that, but her anger brought clarity. They needed to do something.

"Where could they have taken him?" she asked the pack. No one answered, but no one looked away. They watched as the alpha dominated. Her pheromones were overwhelming.

Timmons had already been on the receiving end of being unhelpful. He and the others were ready to do her bidding. All she had to do was command it.

Cordelia was there, along with the rest of the pack. They simply stood in silence and watched, wondering what to do next.

"How did they know where TH was going to be?" Char wondered. She steeled herself, standing up straight. She remembered a tidbit of Terry Henry wisdom. *If you lack information, get it.* "Spread out, run the perimeter and find someone who saw something, find if they used technology, find out how they knew! You have one hour. Go."

Cordelia waited while the others conferred and then, at Were speed, they ran in separate directions, heading for the town's border to search for people and things.

"We'll find him. If it's the last thing we do, we'll find him," Cory said softly as she rubbed her mother's arm.

Char nodded, her features set. No tears. No crippling angst. Heat burned within her like a volcano ready to erupt. Her mind was clear and focused.

"Take this," she said, handing the communication device to Cory. "I'm going to see Jonas and then Joseph. Send up a flare if you hear from Akio. Have him bring at least one pod and all the Earth-searching horsepower at his disposal. I will return as soon as I see your signal. I know we'll find him. If I have to kill every living creature between here and hell, I'll do it to get him back."

Cory nodded, although she didn't agree. She did not want to see her beautiful mother rampage across the countryside, killing innocents as she went. The young woman knew that the Werewolf would leave no skin unshredded as she searched if it came to that.

Char stripped, tied her clothes into a tight bundle, and then changed into a brown-pelted Werewolf, lean and majestic. She grabbed the clothes bundle in her jaws and dashed away.

Please don't kill everyone, Cory begged in a whisper as she rubbed the fur on her ears, a nervous habit that she'd had her whole life.

❖ ❖ ❖

BEIJING

The Forsaken had been raising their heads at inconvenient places and inconvenient times. It was Akio's place to stop them.

Akio was in China, the place that had been demanding more and more of his time. They were breeding Weretigers and creating more Forsaken.

Akio had found himself rushing from one crisis to another. He hesitated to use the Force de Guerre because the issues were small with minimal numbers of Forsaken involved. Akio found it easiest to take care of them himself.

But they were becoming increasingly complex, almost as if the Forsaken were sacrificing their own in order to find the tipping point where they could overwhelm Akio, maybe take on the FDG directly.

Not this time, Akio thought.

The pod landed, opened, and Akio faded into the darkness. The ten-story building on the outskirts of Beijing was being used by yet another Forsaken, building yet another stronghold from which to harvest humanity.

Akio couldn't allow that.

Four guards watched, three on the ground outside and one on the roof. Akio slipped soundlessly through the urban sprawl, stopping when his communication device vibrated ever so gently. Without looking at it, he shut the device down. He would turn it on when he finished cleaning out the hornet's nest.

The first man never knew that someone else was there, a shadow hidden within the blackness of night. A crushing throat punch, followed by a hand clamped tightly over the man's mouth. The guard spasmed as his muscles demanded oxygen that would never come.

The man died kicking against the ground as he lost control of his legs. Akio froze, then gently laid the body to the side and hurried toward his next victim.

The second man died in the same way, in the shadows, with no voice to cry for help, wondering until the end of his life what had happened.

The third man knew something had happened when he expected to cross paths with the others during his rounds and they were nowhere to be seen. He shouted to the man on the roof in Chinese. "Sound the alarm!"

Akio heard the men yelling. He pulled his katana from its saya, its scabbard, and ran toward the third man. He saw the movement and lowered his spear, but it was too late. Akio was past, and his sword had already bitten deeply, rending the man from shoulder to belly.

The man jerked as he flopped to the ground in disbelief at how quickly he was going to die.

Akio moved to the side of the building, and as gracefully as a dancer on the stage, he climbed the building. Over one hundred feet into the air, he continued until he vaulted over the retaining wall and onto the roof. He crouched low to keep from further silhouetting himself. The guard had been looking over the other side. Akio ran, his footfalls making no sound on the light sandy gravel of the roof.

When the man turned, Akio's blade embedded itself in

his body. Twisting and turning, Akio finished the guard, pulling his sword free. He headed for the roof's door without looking back.

Before he opened the door, he reached out, found the Forsaken, the acolytes, and the victims. His lip curled as he fought to maintain his external calm. He loosened his shoulders and narrowed his eyes as he turned the knob and prepared to go to work.

❖ ❖ ❖

NORTH CHICAGO

"You tell me what you heard!" Gene demanded, pounding on the door frame. A family lived on the edge of town, maintaining a small garden and two horses that they used to travel back and forth to the real farms to the west.

The young man looked alarmed while his children cowered in fear. Many in the community had never gotten used to Gene because of his size and rough manners.

"What happened again?" the man asked, leaning away from Gene as if expecting a blow from the Werebear's massive fists.

"Colonel Terry has been taken by bad people flying an air vehicle of some sort," Gene said in his heavy Russian accent. "It was not far. You heard something. You tell me now!"

The man tried to shut the door, but Gene punched it. Aaron appeared behind him and tried to work his way in where Gene would see him before Gene did anything untoward.

"I'm sorry, good sir," Aaron said pleasantly, taller than Gene but a sapling compared to a redwood's trunk. "If you heard or saw anything in the pre-dawn, we would really like to know."

"Nothing. We were sleeping," the man replied, never taking his eyes from Gene.

"The lady of the house? Maybe your children?" Aaron pressed.

The man turned to look inside the aging structure. "Wait, what?" he asked someone within. A woman appeared, with straggly hair, brown eyes, and an expression of perpetual interest.

"I heard something. One man yelling in the dawn. Usually, it's so quiet out here, that's what woke me up," she offered in a faint voice.

Aaron slapped Gene on the arm before the Werebear chased her away. "Only one man was yelling? No one else?" Aaron wondered.

"Yes, only Terry Henry," she answered.

"You know it was him for a fact?"

"Pretty sure." She inched closer to the door with the greater interest that Aaron was taking in her words.

"What did he say?" Aaron focused like a laser beam on her.

"I couldn't hear the words, not all of them, but there were plenty of F-Bombs. I'm sure of that!" she said proudly.

Gene snickered. "Of course he drop fuck bomb. He did not go down without fight."

"Terry's dead?" the man blurted, eyes wide as he tried to get his head wrapped around what the two were saying.

"No!" Gene exclaimed, waving his hands wildly as the conversation wasn't helping him and there were others in the area that he wanted to talk with. "He was taken by bad men with an airplane. You had to hear airplane?"

"Nope," the man replied, relaxing since Terry wasn't dead. He, like everyone else in town, considered Terry Henry Walton to be invincible. If he were only taken, then they wouldn't worry because he would not treat them kindly.

"Bah!" Gene threw his hands up in disgust and stormed away, almost mowing Aaron down as he passed.

"Thank you, both. Wish us luck!" Aaron said with a smile before walking away.

The story was the same from the rest. Everybody heard something. No one saw anything. No one did anything.

And that was how Terry Henry was taken. How many times in the past thirty years had Colonel Walton shown up and saved the day? It was his way. But when his time came, when he needed help, everyone slept soundly in the secure bubble that he'd created for them.

He was condemned to fight alone.

After the last house, Gene changed into his Werebear form so he could stand and roar his anger, demand vengeance, and beg forgiveness.

Crashing through the brush, a graying face appeared.

"Bogdan," Aaron whispered. The two bears nuzzled, and Gene changed back into human form so he could hug his friend. The grizzly weighed in at nearly eight hundred pounds. He'd been with humans nearly his whole life, so he wasn't a threat to them. The people of North Chicago looked at him as the town mascot. He and the elephant Jumbo held special places within the community.

Bogdan wasn't sporting the lean muscle of a wild bear, but he could hunt and take care of himself.

Like the time he got into the Weathers' cow pasture.

"You are lucky you survived that one, my son," Gene told him.

"You need to get your clothes on," Aaron said, averting his eyes from the big man.

"What for? This is Grade A prime beef!" Gene bellowed, beating on his chest like a gorilla. Bogdan mirrored the big man's motions.

"Clothes!" Aaron insisted.

❖ ❖ ❖

TERRY'S PRISON

Someone opened the door and entered. Without raising his head, Terry looked up from under his brow. He tracked the newcomer until the door closed, cutting off the little light from the hallway beyond.

"I can smell you," Terry whispered, listening with every fiber of his being. He could hear his own heartbeat. The newcomer moved almost as quietly as a butterfly, but the slight rustle of clothing gave him away.

Terry leaned back against his chains, rotating his shoulder as he stretched onto his tiptoes. It popped back into the socket with an audible thump. He gasped, but already his augmented nanocytes were at work.

Char, you are the best thing that has ever happened to me. You make life worth living, he thought as if in prayer.

The newcomer stopped moving, becoming a hole in the empty space of the room.

A Forsaken, listening in to Terry's mind.

Char, I love you so, Terry continued, letting his thoughts return to the sailboat and the open lake, two days away from North Chicago. They'd made love on the deck, sailed naked until they made love again. Under the cerulean sky on water so deep blue, it looked black, a light breeze flapping against the sail. They didn't care to make any speed. They were where they were meant to be.

"Char," Terry whispered in the lightness of breath.

He heard the creature only inches from his face.

Terry lunged, driving his forehead at the Forsaken's face. The Vampire was caught unaware; his nose shattered and flattened against his face. Terry pulled himself up until his legs were off the ground. He hooked the creature's leg as it was falling backward.

He dragged the Forsaken to him and stomped on its head. Mercilessly, he continued. "You don't deserve to see her, not in my mind. Not anywhere."

Terry crushed the Forsaken's head and kept driving his boot heel into it until its brains were scattered across the floor.

The door opened and Kirkus entered. He turned on the lights.

"A sailboat, very creative lovemaking, TH. I think we need to bring this woman to us. The sacrifice of this one, I think, was well worth those images, my friend. Oh, how those purple eyes sparkle," the Forsaken taunted.

Terry Henry glared at Kirkus and imagined all manners of ways in which he would kill the Forsaken.

All manners.

Kirkus stared back, refusing to be intimidated. The world was his to take, not Terry Henry Walton's. Not a different Forsaken. Not anyone but him.

Gilbert Kirkus planned years in advance. The world didn't know who he was, but they would. Soon enough, they all would know. With purple eyes by his side, no one could stand before him. Then he'd make his move to take over what had been the United States, and then he'd expand to the rest of the world.

He chuckled to himself. His plans were finally coming to fruition.

Terry saw a wisp of madness pass across the Forsaken's eyes. In an instant, it was gone, and the eyes were cold once again. It wasn't time to challenge the creature.

Terry looked at the stinking corpse on the floor. He'd seen worse, but not by much. He turned his attention to Kirkus. "Sorry about your minion, there, fuckstick, but not really. He was a fuckstick, too. As a matter of fact, you can't swing a dead cat around here without hitting a fuckstick. It's like a fuckstick farm--just when you harvest one, another pops up in its place. Would you look at that? Just when we thought we stomped the living shit out of a fuckstick, its twin fuckstick brother shows up. I'll be damned."

"You will indeed be damned, Terry Henry Walton, by me and me alone. Your living hell has only just begun." Kirkus walked away casually, ignoring the body on the floor. He turned off the lights and shut the door slowly, darkening the room one agonizing inch at a time, until total darkness returned.

Terry heard Kirkus laughing as he walked away.

CHAPTER THREE

Akio saw them clearly in his mind: five Forsaken and six humans, two of which were kept for their blood, although by Forsaken logic, any human life was forfeit if the Forsaken were hungry enough.

Not today, Akio thought as he descended the stairs, silent as a ghost.

The most dangerous Forsaken was on the top floor. Akio decided to forego the stealth approach and walked into the hallway and toward the room where his enemy would be found. The Forsaken was pacing.

Akio opened the door casually and walked in. He was surprised to see a westerner.

"My name is unimportant," the Forsaken started with a dismissive wave. "I expect you are the famous Akio, slayer of my kind. A shame. We didn't choose to be what we are. That decision was made for us, and we have to live with it, the best we can."

Akio didn't reply. He kept his distance as he took stock of the room, noting the furniture, tripping hazards, possible traps.

Despite his words, the unnamed one carried a long curved blade with an ivory grip. A filigree was engraved down the blade. Akio had only seen one other like it. A Mameluke, the sword carried by United States Marine officers in the before time.

The kaleidoscopic color of the steel suggested it was a Damascus blade, one of the very best.

Akio's appreciation of his enemy's steel was limited to what he needed to do to kill the creature and then move through the building to eliminate the rest. Akio still didn't say anything because there was nothing to say. He gripped his katana in both hands as he approached, sidestepping without crossing his feet.

He shifted from right to left, looking for the side that the Forsaken favored. The unnamed didn't give it away. He smoothly matched Akio's moves.

The first blow came as each swung toward the head of the other. Akio turned his blade slightly to catch the cutting edge of the Mameluke on the flat of his blade, letting it slide the length and past his head. Akio ducked low and swung low, diving to the side as he saw the glint of a redirected slash.

The unnamed barely missed Akio, but the master Japanese swordsman's aim was true. The tip of his katana tore through the Forsaken's thigh, slicing a notch into the femur as it passed. Blood spurted from the sliced artery.

Akio returned upright and bounced away, ready for a counterstrike.

But the Forsaken held his leg with one hand, backing up slowly. He twirled his sword in front of him, carving a figure eight in the air. Akio saw a door, and he ran at the unnamed.

The Forsaken turned to bolt, but his leg betrayed him and he stumbled. Akio's first slash removed the Forsaken's sword arm. In less than a blink of the eye, the unnamed's head was rolling on the floor. The body remained upright for a moment, then toppled.

Akio looked at the blade on the floor. He picked it up and studied it briefly. A fitting sword for a man he would call a friend. Akio cleaned it on the couch, then drove it home into its silver and gold scabbard. He slipped it next to the katana's saya and hurried into the corridor and toward the steps.

❖ ❖ ❖

CHICAGO

"My! What brings you to my doorstep?" Jonas said warmly to the purple-eyed Werewolf standing before him. She was still in Were form. She dropped her clothes bundle and changed into human form.

Jonas leered at her. "You decided that you needed a real man, that the human couldn't satisfy you?"

She stopped reaching for her clothes, frozen for an instant, before rotating and driving the heel of her hand into his chest. He flew backwards, crashing into a wall.

Char didn't bother with her clothes. She launched herself at him, pounding his face with punch after punch. She pulled him to his feet so she could step back and send a sidekick into his belly button that slammed him against the wall a second time. With a spinning roundhouse that caught him on the side of his head, he went down.

She dressed while she waited impatiently for him to wake

up. His eyes fluttered, and she pulled him roughly to his feet and slammed him against the wall.

"You always were a limp dick piece of shit, Jonas. I should probably just kill you, but first, I need to know why you did it. Tell me!" she demanded.

"What do you think I did?" he stammered.

"Sold us out, you whiny bitch. I want to know why. And while you're telling, I want to know where they took him." Char emphasized her question by slamming the Werewolf into the wall.

"Who did I sell out?" he asked, clearly confused.

Char started to believe it wasn't him, but she was certain he'd done something to deserve a beating. He always deserved to have his ass kicked.

She let him go. "A dozen Forsaken flew in here and took Terry Henry prisoner. They escaped before we could get to them. I know you're in bed with the evil of this world. You had something to do with it, because that's the fucked up shit that you do."

She jabbed a finger into his chest hard enough to make him wince. She felt gratified seeing him in pain. She did it again, smiling at his anguish.

"Although I'll be the first to congratulate the sonofabitch that kills your husband, I had nothing to do with this. If you find them, let me know. Tell them the first round is on me," Jonas sneered.

Char had had enough. She turned into him with her arm raised, fist in hand as she rocketed her elbow into his face, crushing the bones beneath. She punched him twice for good measure. He didn't go down until she kneed him in the groin hard enough to lift him off his feet. He landed in a crumpled pile, barely breathing but alive.

He'd live. Char shrugged, removed her clothes, and changed into Were form for the long run to downtown Chicago in search of the Forsaken, Joseph.

◈ ◈ ◈

TERRY'S PRISON

Terry didn't know how long he had hung there. He'd put himself into a higher state of calm through meditation to give the nanocytes an easier path to do what they needed to do to repair his injuries. But he hadn't eaten or drank anything for too long. His nanocytes needed the energy to continue their work.

He thought about eating the shriveled Forsaken on the floor, but decided he wasn't hungry enough for that, probably would never be that hungry.

TH couldn't remember the last time he'd been truly hungry. He remembered the last time he'd eaten too much. That was just last week. He and Char were visiting the ranch that Auburn and Kimber ran. They had bred the livestock over the past twenty-five years and had a massive herd, many produced with the longhorns that Eli had provided out of Wyoming.

Kimber and Auburn. He remembered the day he saw them holding hands. She was eleven and he thought the Weathers boy was twelve at the time. They were friends long before they became adults and fell in love.

"Auburn! Your brother Clemson isn't even in the Southeastern Conference!" Terry shouted to the empty room. Terry shook his head, rattling the heavy chains attached to the shackles on his wrists. "Antioch. Even after you snagged your seat on the great rocking chair in the sky, you are still messing with me. Well done, my man, well done."

TH shifted, flexed, and stretched as much as he could. The nanocytes were working overtime. He was starting to feel more like his old self. Whatever they hit him with to get him into the pod, it was finally wearing off.

"If you're listening, Kirky-poo, I could use a drink of some agua fria. Being healthy will make your torture last so much longer. You don't want me to die while you're pleasuring yourself, do you?" Terry chuckled as he grabbed the chains and pulled, rocking back and forth, pulling, working at the eyebolts set into the wall.

They didn't move, but it looked like he had time. In the darkness, he strained against the chains. He flexed and pulled.

Not bad for an eighty-five-year-old man, he thought. The cords of his thick muscles stood out along his arms and back. He grunted with the effort, but nothing moved.

Not yet anyway.

❖ ❖ ❖

NORTH CHICAGO

Timmons ran into the motor pool. Resources were dwindling, but they were at the forefront of a second industrial revolution. The newest vehicles were better than a Model T, but the engineering was as simple. It was Timmons and Shonna's design.

They hadn't had any problems with the engines and transmissions, but the tires were still giving them fits.

Timmons looked at the newest four vehicles, which looked like an old Willys Jeep.

Corporal Heitz leaned heavily on his cane as he limped forward to greet the engineer. First Sergeant Blevin joined him, walking gingerly but without help. The oldsters no longer ran the motor pool, but they had nowhere else to go, so they hung out and made life hell for the young mechanics.

Timmons didn't waste any time. "The colonel's been taken by a mob of Forsaken. They took him away in an aircraft of some sort. Did any of you guys see anything?"

"I'm lucky if I can see the sun rise," Max Heitz responded coldly. "But if I sure as hell heard anything, I'd tell you. But I didn't."

Blevin shook his head. The motor pool was on the other side of their community, opposite where Terry had been attacked.

"We want to go," Max stated, shuffling close to Timmons and looking up into his face. "On the rescue. You are going, right?"

"We can't get a hold of Akio, for some reason. I'm afraid we're dead in the water, Max. We're asking everyone if they saw anything. We don't even know which direction they went when they flew away. We need to be able to start looking somewhere and we got nothing!" Timmons shared sadly.

"Ain't that a ballbuster? When you do go, we're going, too. These babies will fit in those pods of yours. We can take one, haul our old carcasses around the battlefield. One last romp, eh, Blevin?"

"One last romp," the first sergeant repeated in an old voice.

"Mount the fifty, Blevin. We're going to war!" Max called in a freshly energized voice.

"We haven't been able to get a hold of Akio!" Timmons exclaimed, trying to get the old men's attention. "No one is going anywhere."

"We have faith. You'll get a hold of him and Akio will come. Then we'll go get our colonel. Who'd you say had him?" Max asked.

"The Forsaken. They overwhelmed him and took him away," Timmons explained.

"A temporary state of affairs. The reason they took the colonel and didn't just kill him is because he's invincible. They can't kill him. They'll try to lock him up, but that won't work either. We'll probably just go pick him up as he'll have already killed them all. We'll know where to go because of the funeral pyre lighting the sky. He'll make them pay alright. But we had best not make him wait. Lug my ma deuce over here, Blevin!" Heitz was on a roll.

Blevin raised his eyebrows skeptically. He had neither the desire nor strength to carry the fifty-caliber machine gun by himself.

Timmons elbowed his way past them to the motor pool's weapons locker and recovered the fifty cal. He carried it to the jeep and mounted it for the two old men.

"Remember the last time we used that big bastard?" Heitz asked.

"Oh yeah," Blevins said with a crooked smile.

"Stupid fuckers thought they were going to land that old boat of theirs right here on our beach!" Max cackled like an old man. Blevin was older, but Max had it worse inside Cheyenne Mountain. They never talked about their twenty years trapped with the Forsaken. They only talked about the good times afterwards, brought to them by Terry Henry Walton.

"I think the colonel was mad that he didn't get to fire the big gun," Blevin suggested.

The men had rehashed the incident a thousand times since it happened. A boat came from nowhere with rough looking men carrying bows. They made the mistake of coming too close and firing an arrow at Corporal Heitz.

It took no time for the men of the motor pool to bring the M2 to bear. They blew the small boat and the intruders out of the water.

The hulk was still on the bottom a hundred yards out, in the shallower water. "Fuck those pussies," Heitz said.

"It's Darwin, my friend. Darwin naturally selected those knuckleheads to end their participation in the gene pool. Thank you for playing. Next!" Blevin bellowed.

The two men howled, until a racking cough seized Corporal Heitz. Blevin beat on his back while Max tried to push him away. It was a routine they'd done often.

Max wiped a mouth on his sleeve, then headed for the passenger seat. He couldn't see well enough to drive, so Blevin took the wheel. After a couple turns, the engine coughed to life, belching acrid black smoke.

"We need to fix that," Timmons offered. A ring was shot, and one of the cylinders was burning oil. "Why don't you take number four?"

The two old men waved their hands at Timmons, gunning the jeep and working up to second gear as they drove from the motor pool. Timmons watched them go, wondering what he'd accomplished.

❖ ❖ ❖

Sue was leaving Claire's Diner when she caught sight of Kimber and Kaeden running toward the barracks. The grim expressions on their faces told Sue that something was up. She changed course and intercepted them.

After a quick recap, Kae headed inside the building,

taking a left and going straight to the weapons locker, the second to last room on the first floor. Captain Mark occupied the last room and oversaw the logistics for the FDG. He was no longer active with the troops.

That was a young person's game, but the Force couldn't go anywhere or do anything without support. The FDG also maintained a storage building behind the barracks. It was chock-full of weapons and equipment.

As the colonel always said, amateurs talk tactics, professionals talk logistics. Mark had been a professional with the FDG for nearly thirty years.

He was up and already dressed. He had the armory open and was working on one of the rifles. They were still fully stocked on ammunition because they made regular trips back to Cheyenne Mountain. They had been incrementally emptying its supplies. Once the survivors had been rescued, all maintenance on the vehicles had stopped. They looked good sitting in those tunnels, but none of them were ever going to leave the darkness of their tomb.

The ammunition and weapons would last forever in that kind of environment. After all this time, there was still a stock, but it was getting low. The FDG had used more than they would admit.

Mark removed and cleaned the glasses that someone had found somewhere. He said they helped him to see like an eagle.

The others weren't sure, but no one made fun of the captain. You wouldn't get your ammunition issued and then you wouldn't be able to join a deployment. Mark held the power of logistics and used it as a finely honed instrument to shape the warriors as they needed to be shaped.

He listened carefully as Kimber told the tale. Mark's

expression didn't change. He nodded when Kim finished, putting the disassembled rifle to the side. He looked at the racks, lips moving as he took inventory, although he knew it all by heart. It was his routine.

It was what he always did before a deployment, because when the FDG deployed, it was to fight an enemy. Sometimes the enemy surrendered, but most of the time, they decided to fight. Combat was the worst time to find out that the warriors were missing something they needed.

Mark flexed his trunk, grimacing as the old wound acted up. He clenched his teeth to power through the pain.

"Still hurt?" Sue asked. She'd been there when it happened. Adams had jumped in to carry the lieutenant out of the line of fire.

One of the warriors had bandaged his wounds. He refused Cory's help, because there were those who were worse off and her influence was limited.

Mark nodded.

"Honor, before all things," he replied proudly. Terry Henry Walton had made him and the Force de Guerre the symbol of the oppressed, the bane of would-be dictators. "When do we leave?"

"I don't know, but Mom wants you to be ready to deploy," Kae responded.

"We'll meet you in Mayor's Park in fifteen minutes. All of us," Mark said. He followed them out of the armory, making them jump when he yelled down the hallway for an emergency callout of the entire Force.

"What's up, Captain?" someone called.

"We're going to war, ladies. Out in front in ten, now MOVE!" Mark bellowed.

CHAPTER FOUR

TERRY'S PRISON

Terry breathed slowly and rhythmically, feeling the strength returning to his body. He squinted and concentrated, finally able to make out the crack under the door where one or two lumens crept past. Despite his best efforts, he could see nothing else in the room.

He kicked at the dead body, now shriveled to a mere husk of its former self. Terry kicked it away from him so he wouldn't have to touch it.

In the silence, he heard footsteps, hard soles on a hard floor, clickety clack.

It wasn't Kirkus, unless he'd swapped his soft-sole slippers for cowboy boots.

The door was thrown open and the light turned on. Terry blinked and squinted against the brightness. Kirkus stood next to an incredibly beautiful Chinese woman, tall and shapely, skin like alabaster. Her oversized almond-shaped eyes were dark as she visually explored the body of Terry Henry Walton.

"How nice of you to bring your pet kitty," Terry said in a low voice, tensing with the expectation of what she was there to do.

Kirkus stepped aside without a word. The young-looking woman started to undress, slowly, seductively. A lesser man may have been lulled into enjoying the show, but with each article of clothing removed, she was one step closer to turning into a Weretiger.

TH couldn't defend himself. He'd seen Aaron in Were form too many times to count and knew the damage that would be wrought by a Weretiger's claws.

Kirkus chuckled softly to himself, but didn't tell the woman to hurry. He was enjoying the anticipation of pain that filled Terry's mind.

Once fully naked, she turned one way and then another to show her curves and her pride in her body. Terry only saw the muscles of a fighter. He closed his eyes for a moment, trying to block her out while all the muscles in his body tensed.

When he felt hot breath on his face, he opened his eyes and found himself face-to-face with the orange-furred Weretiger. He didn't try to head-butt her; she was just out of range. He remained still while she sniffed him.

He saw her eye twitch as a paw blurred in how quickly it raked its claws across his stomach. He didn't feel it at first, then it was like fire burning through his skin and into his very soul.

The Weretiger stalked back and forth, sizing up her prey while TH worked through the pain. He chanced a look, saw the shredded skin and torn muscle beneath.

Terry consoled himself with believing that Kirkus needed

him alive for some reason. Otherwise, they wouldn't be playing games.

"Damn, kitten. Look what you did to my beach body?" Terry taunted, flexing himself in anticipation of another slash. She jumped up and he flinched.

She landed with the pads of her paws on his shoulders. She was heavy and his shoulders screamed with the strain. The shackles dug deeply into his wrists.

The Weretiger leaned close. Her feline eyes studied him. She licked his face from chin to forehead with her wide and raspy tongue.

"Come on, kitten. You've been eating too much ass lately. Maybe try a breath mint every now and again," Terry grumbled.

She sniffed and nuzzled his face, then nibbled his ear. He froze. She clamped down, driving a fang through the cartilage.

Terry gasped, but didn't cry out. His stomach hurt more than his ear. He decided not to taunt her further and forced himself to relax.

She spun and slapped his knee with a paw, then did it again, much harder the second time and with her claws out. He lost his balance and hopped on one leg to take the weight off his shoulders.

She stalked away, changing into her human form. She bent at the waist to put her shoes on, then gathered her clothes, carrying them in her arm as she walked naked from the room, clickety-clacking into the hallway beyond the door.

Kirkus held the door for her. Neither of them had said a single word.

Blood ran down Terry's stomach, drenching his shorts. Drips were starting to build into a puddle on the floor.

"I suggest you not kill this one if you wish to eat and drink," Kirkus said over a shoulder as he walked away. The light was still on in the room. TH would have wondered except moments later, a minion entered. *Female*, Terry thought, but not completely certain.

She brought a tray of food and a pitcher of water. He smacked his dry lips, barely able to keep his eyes open as his nanocytes were taking energy from anywhere they could find it, making him unnaturally tired.

The minion held the pitcher to his lips and he drank, swallowing heavily as it had been awhile and his throat was parched. She was much shorter than Terry and held the jug at arm's length over her head, trying to control the flow. The water dribbled over his face when he couldn't keep up.

"Food, please," he said, but she shook her head. He didn't know where she came from, but she looked Asian. He suspected she didn't speak English so he pointed with his chin and eyes. She handed him the first bite, then the second, until the tray was empty.

Terry felt like he could have eaten a horse, but what she gave him was all he was going to get. She poured the rest of the pitcher into his mouth, bowed and started to leave.

"Thank you," he said, before digging into his mind and pulling out the Mandarin words and then the Cantonese words. "Xie xie. M goi." She nodded slightly as she walked out, closing the door behind herself. She did him the courtesy of leaving the light on.

❖ ❖ ❖

Akio saw four humans coming toward him. They carried short spears. He pulled one pistol and shot them, one by one. They never knew that they didn't stand a chance. Akio holstered his pistol, one of two that he always carried and rarely used.

The Forsaken stepped into the hallway on the first floor of the building. He was the last, and he knew it. Like the rest, he was arrogant enough to believe he had a chance against the sword master.

The man pulled two short blades from behind his back. They looked like the Elven blades from *Lord of the Rings*. Akio cocked his head, wondering if they were real.

The man sauntered past the human bodies. He didn't waste time looking at them as he sized up his enemy. He whirled his blades and moved close.

Akio waited while the Forsaken continued his intricate sword dance.

The katana whistled past the Forsaken's dipped blade. The curved blade bit deeply into the creature's neck. A second swing cleanly removed the Forsaken's head.

Akio crouched in the ready position, weaving his blade through the air around him as he explored the etheric looking for more enemies. None remained.

He wiped his blade clean on the clothes of his enemy, examined its length for nicks, and then sent the blade home.

Akio walked with a purpose to the room where the prisoners were being kept. He opened the door, walked in, released them, and left. He didn't say anything as he left them to themselves.

Akio strolled from the modern building on the outskirts

of what used to be Beijing, stopping to look at the city's lights in the distance. Power had been restored in enclaves around the world, serving the city-states in which the plants could be found.

City-states had been combined to form loose nation-states. Transportation was still iffy at best, but the trains were running in many areas and made up the only form of long-distance travel. The people still did not have high-speed air travel fifty years after the world's worst day ever (WWDE).

On rare occasions, blimps could be seen making their way through the skies. Akio had almost hit one as the pod flew itself to the designated landing coordinates on this trip.

He looked up into the darkness. The stars winked back at him. The air had cleared after the WWDE as pollutants stopped being sent skyward. Beijing had been one of the worst cities on the planet. Now, it was like the others, boasting clean air and crystal clear skies overhead.

There was minimal light pollution to cloud the view.

Almost like home, Akio thought. *Almost.*

The pod opened as Akio approached, his mission complete. It was time to go home.

He stopped and looked back at the building, wondering why this bunch had exposed themselves as they did, becoming a flashing red light on his map of emergencies.

He sat down within, pulling out his communication device and turning it back on. Char had tried three times to contact him, which was three more times than she'd called in the past twenty-five years.

He immediately activated a call to her.

"Akio?" a young-sounding voice replied.

"Cordelia? You called me?" Akio asked softly.

"No, it was my mother. You must come at once and bring

all the pods! Forsaken have taken Father. They took him away in an aircraft of some sort. We need to find him!" Cory pleaded, her detached voice coming through the device loud and clear.

"When?"

"Maybe two hours ago? Maybe a little longer," she replied.

"I will be there shortly. Be ready," Akio told her before signing off.

❖ ❖ ❖

NORTH CHICAGO

Ted stood in the power plant's parking lot. He had run from the center of North Chicago, past the perimeter of the community. He'd continued all the way to the plant.

There were too many people doing too many different things in the town. It was crushing him, and he panted in distress.

He had to get away, even though he expected his alpha would be annoyed. His pack was with him. Several generations removed from his original pack, the timber wolves had all grown up knowing Ted as their alpha. They lived their lives and they passed on. The latest pack had wolves up to eight generations from the first pack he'd taken over near the Rocky Mountains.

The pack had split a few times when it had grown too large. As it was, the current pack of twenty-three wolves ate a great deal of food, but big game was migrating from Canada, close enough to keep everyone happy without the wolves digging into the herd of cattle. Or waiting on the shore for one of the fishing boats to return.

Ted absentmindedly walked among his pack, not having to bend over to scratch their heads. An outsider would have had a heart attack from fear, but Ted and the insiders of North Chicago considered the wolf pack to be family.

He moved through the meandering beasts to his baby, looking shiny and new.

The Mini Cooper modular nuclear reactor. They'd only had to refuel seven times in twenty-five years. The original design called for refueling every two years, but Ted knew they could get more mileage from the system. At the beginning, they didn't need to burn so hot that they expended the rods in two years. He'd been able to stretch the operation to four years on the original fueling before they had to search for more fuel rods.

With Akio's help, they found replacement fuel rods in cold storage. With a minimal number of reactors running in the new world, there were sufficient rods for hundreds of years of operation. Ted thought beyond that and had talked with Terry about establishing a new uranium mine and fuel processing facility.

Terry had nodded but refused to work with the mayor to commit any resources to such a venture. He told Ted that it was added to the long-term needs list.

Ted smiled, thinking of how he'd managed the reaction over the years with limited computer resources. He'd done many of the calculations in his head, because he could. No one could do what he could, but he didn't brag.

That wasn't what Ted was about. His was a constant internal struggle with the math. Equations bombarded him like he was standing in a pouring rain. He needed to answer the problem, and then move to the next. There was a never-ending stream.

Ted saw the flare arc into the sky over North Chicago. He saw it but it didn't register. The Mini Cooper was calling his name. It needed an adjustment. He climbed the ladder that he'd climbed thousands of times before. He closed his eyes as he caressed the control panel. He could see everything within his mind.

He opened his eyes to look at the numbers. He tweaked a couple settings, estimating an efficiency improvement of a thousandth of one percent. Not much, but better.

Ted always did better, especially when it came to math.

The wolves were scattered in a parking lot devoid of vehicles. They lounged on the concrete, soaking up the heat. Ted was tired. He climbed down the ladder and laid down with his pack, making himself comfortable against their shaggy coats as he went to sleep.

CHAPTER FIVE

CHICAGO

Char sensed something behind her. She turned her Werewolf head to see a flare rocketing into the early morning sky. The green light slowly descended, the parachute above it invisible.

She was both relieved and angry. She had not yet found Joseph and she wanted to talk with him, recruit him to go along.

The flare meant that Akio had been in touch, was maybe even on his way. Char hadn't told Cory to wait for her, an oversight on Char's part.

She had to decide.

Char turned and ran toward the tallest building of the downtown, picking up speed with each stride. She didn't care if she was seen. None of that mattered as long as Terry Henry Walton was missing.

She reached out with her senses as she ran, looking for

the Forsaken that she grudgingly called a friend. Terry had seen the potential in Joseph when they first met. He'd given Joseph a chance and from then on, the Forsaken had been one of Terry's team.

He'd been one of the pack, the ultimate tactical team. They'd never failed in a mission, although they'd left bits and pieces of themselves behind. They'd even lost one of their own. In Cheyenne Mountain, Xandrie died at the hands of a Forsaken. In China, Gene almost died after a fight with a Weretiger.

Since then, Terry had spent a great deal of time turning the wrestler into a fighter, helping him understand how best to use his strengths while limiting his weaknesses. He no longer allowed an opponent to get close.

Char couldn't help thinking about him. Her mind started to drift.

"As big as that fucking melon is on your shoulders, you'd think there'd be a fucking brain in there bigger than a fucking walnut!" Terry had yelled. No one wanted to see Gene injured like that again.

Char realized that she was trotting. The flare was long gone. She bolted forward, picking up speed.

She was relieved when she sensed the Forsaken. He was a few stories below ground and that had been blocking his presence. She stopped in an alley, changed back into human form, and dressed.

When she walked back into the street, three young punks were there, knives out, and ready to go after the big dog they'd seen just a few moments earlier.

❖ ❖ ❖

Terry's mouth was dry again, but the food and water he'd been given earlier was providing the energy his nanocytes needed. He flexed to lean down and look, finding that the wound on his stomach had closed. His muscles were still sore, but he was recovering.

"How long are we going to keep this up?" he asked the empty room. Terry flexed his knee and found that it could support his weight again. He started working his shoulders and pulling on the chains, rocking back and forth.

His wrists were sore, but he pushed the pain out of his mind. He thought about the history of prisoners of war, those who were taken in Vietnam and returned alive after up to nine years in the harshest of conditions.

They were emaciated, but they smiled as they walked toward freedom. Terry recalled the video footage in great detail. He remembered every word of the biographies--Captain Floyd Thompson, the longest held American POW ever. Nine years in captivity. How much of his life was wasted behind the bars of a North Vietnamese prison?

Terry chased the thoughts away, gritting his teeth to strain against his chains. Work them a little at a time. Every minute of every day, he would pull on the eyebolts until they started to give, then he would redouble his efforts and tear them from the wall.

He thought back to the images in his mind of the survivors. He decided that he would rather die trying to escape.

Terry Henry Walton was okay with disappointing his captor. Stockholm syndrome? No. With each passing second, he only wanted to kill the Forsaken that much more.

❖ ❖ ❖

"Where's Mother?" Cory asked impatiently. Felicity shook her head. Billy tried to calm her down.

"She'll be here when she needs to be here," Billy said slowly in his rough, gravelly voice. "Your mother isn't going to abandon TH. You know that she's doing what she needs to be doing for your father."

Cory looked at the old man seated in a rocking chair. The sound of dogs barking filled the air.

Dogs were always barking in North Chicago. Clyde's descendants were every bit as vocal and happy as the old coonhound had been. The dog guaranteed his legacy when he had taken over the pack left behind by the circus-wagon Forsaken.

Cory had only been a baby back then.

A scrappy coonhound-mix pup ran into Mayor's Park and started to squat. "You stop that!" Billy tried to yell before coughing himself silly. Felicity ran after it, but the dog finished his business and ran circles around Felicity. The community had put the tools to clean up the inevitable messes nearby.

The mayor took care of the dog's healthy dump. She looked, but no one was there. She cupped her hands around her mouth and yelled. "Whoever is responsible for that mangy cur, you owe me!"

Cory tried not to make eye contact with the mayor. She walked down the stairs to the mayor's building. The pup ran to her, putting his front paws on her thighs and expecting to get his ears scratched.

"Yours?" Felicity asked, narrowing her eyes.

"Afraid so. I guess I could have stopped you and taken over," she suggested.

"Guess so," Felicity replied, before slapping the taller woman on the back and continuing up the steps.

"Look what you did, Clovis. You got me in trouble with the mayor!" Cory corrected the dog, but in a playful voice. She needed to be stricter, as Sue kept telling her. The pup was eight months old and getting bigger by the minute. She wondered how big he was going to get.

Her father had an innate love for canines of all sorts, dogs or wolves. It didn't matter. "Man's best friend!" Terry would yell from anywhere, usually earning himself a punch from his wife. Cory smiled, thinking of her parents. Her father had been taken and her mother was off on a private mission to find anything or anyone who could help them.

The tears threatened to fall. She wasn't prone to crying. Crying had never helped her with anything. Charumati taught her that physical activity was the cure for tears. That was why Char made such an effective pack leader, the alpha dog, because if she got too frustrated, someone would get their ass kicked.

Cory felt the adrenaline flowing through her veins. She couldn't wait to unleash her anger on those who had caused her family such pain.

❖ ❖ ❖

"Company, Ah-ten-shun!" Mark bellowed, using his diaphragm to project the words in the compound between the barracks and Claire's Diner. The Force de Guerre snapped to attention.

Nearly one hundred men and women were split between four platoons. The only constant was the physical fitness demanded of the Force de Guerre. They needed to be able to function in any environment, carrying any load. Everything else was secondary. From young to old, all shapes and sizes filled the ranks.

"Report!" Lieutenant Blackbeard ordered from his position in front. The platoon sergeants each reported all present. He executed a sharp salute, followed by an about face. He saluted the captain. "All present."

Mark saluted back. He stepped close to Blackbeard. They'd served together a long time, but they were getting older.

"One last hurrah, Blackie," Mark said in a low voice, not wanting the others to hear. "Somebody took the colonel and we need to go get him. Let's see who measures up, see who's next in line to lead these fine warriors."

Blackie didn't move. He was contemplating the fact that Colonel Walton had been taken. "Who could pull that off?" he finally asked.

"Forsaken. The colonel killed eight of them, if I heard right. But Akio will come and get us and then we'll go get him," Mark replied, looking past the lieutenant. "Let me talk to our people."

Blackbeard stepped aside, opening the way for Mark to address the Force.

"Who's up for a rescue mission?" Mark belted out.

Oorahs and cheers answered him.

"The colonel's been taken by a bunch of Forsaken and we need to go get him. Any of you goofy fuckers wanna stay home?" The cheering stopped and there was a brief silence.

"Fuck no!" somebody yelled from within the formation.

Mark would have laughed if the situation hadn't been so dire.

"We have no idea about anything except that Akio will bring the pods. We'll load up everything we can, and then we'll hunt those bastards down."

Mark stepped back. "Platoon Sergeants, front and center," he ordered. The four at the front of the formation hustled to reach the captain. Sergeants Boris, Allen, Allison, and Nickles reported smartly. The platoon sergeants were young, a newer generation of warrior. All of them had been born during the time of the rebuilding.

Gunnery Sergeant Lacy was there, too, as the company gunny. Jim and some of the other originals were in the back row. They were too old or too broken to keep up. They'd surrendered their positions to younger, more capable warriors, but they were always ready to go and for a mission like this, they wouldn't miss it for the world.

"Inspect your people. We need a good variety of weapons and equipment, because we don't know anything. They could be in the greatest fortress known to man or they could be in a paper shack in the middle of the Wasteland. If it's the fortress? We need to be able to breach it. Fix your load out and get ready to move to Mayor's Park and wait for pickup. Questions?"

Nobody had any.

"Go."

Mark pulled Blackie aside as the platoon sergeants got to work. "Nothing is more important than this, Lieutenant," Mark emphasized.

His words were unnecessary. They saluted each other and went their separate ways, each committed to their jobs. Gunnery Sergeant Lacy, affectionately called Gunny in the style of the old Marine Corps, joined Blackie to map out the deployment plan and to inject their own preferences into the equipment load outs.

❖ ❖ ❖

CHICAGO

"Hot mama! What brings you to our side of town?" the first young tough asked, presenting a knife blade and making a show of licking it. The other two laughed and nodded.

"No time for the likes of you. Get the fuck out of my way," Char growled.

"Kiss your baby with that mouth?" the young man taunted. He spoke over his shoulder. "Grab her."

The other two hooted as they rushed in, each heading for an arm. Char was thinking the same thing. She only needed one arm to deal with the likes of them.

She balanced on the balls of her feet, flexing in anticipation. As they came within arm's reach, she rushed forward, grabbing each young man by his throat. Char picked them off the ground and slammed their heads together. She let them both drop to the ground.

"I told you that I had no time. Now take these two and leave this place," she ordered with a half-growl.

The young man wasn't going to give up that easily. He turned the blade point forward and charged. Char dodged the clumsy attack, blocked the knife away from her, and with her follow through, she elbowed the man in the face so hard that it snapped his neck.

His head flopped sideways on his shoulders as his dead body fell across the other two.

"Won't you be surprised when you wake up," she told

them as she ran to the front door, through it, and down the stairs. She'd been there many times before.

She knew the way.

She also knew the code to get into Joseph's chambers, but she didn't need to use it. He was waiting for her. By the time Char arrived six levels down, he was walking toward her, having already explored her mind and seen the urgency.

"There's no time to waste," he told her as he hurried past her. She turned and followed him. They ran up the stairs, through the lobby, and out the door. The three men were where she'd left them.

"Your handiwork?" he asked.

"They were in my way," she replied.

"Clearly," he agreed. Together, they ran like the wind for North Chicago.

CHAPTER SIX

TERRY'S PRISON

Terry pulled himself from his meditation, feeling much better. Kirkus was standing there, looking at him.

"What's for breakfast, huggy muffins?" Terry said casually, not surprised at how silently the Forsaken moved. It didn't matter. Terry couldn't do anything about the Forsaken's movements.

Terry wasn't going to watch the corridor like a psychopath, fixating on the anticipation of the next visit, the next bout of pain that would be inflicted. It was a self-defeating approach, mind and soul-crushing.

And that wasn't how TH lived his life.

"So, you think you can break the eyebolts from the wall?" Kirkus said casually, staying out of his prisoner's reach as he checked the chains and the attachments. "I honestly don't know if you can or not, but I'll keep checking. We simply cannot have you running free in here."

"In here? Where would that be, you warthog-faced buffoon, you miserable vomitous mass?" Terry smiled pleasantly, flexing his shoulders to keep them limber, just in case.

"Honestly, TH, I thought you would be more intellectual than quoting bad movies," Kirkus replied.

Terry rattled his chains. His lip curled and he yelled, "Hey! There's a line that you just don't cross. Why do you have to use such hurtful words?"

Terry chuckled at his joke.

Kirkus spun and kicked the prisoner in the abdomen, where the muscles were still knitting back together. Terry gasped and fought the urge to power puke. He calmed his breathing. As soon as he took his second slow, deep breath, the Forsaken kicked him again.

There wasn't much of Terry's meal remaining in his stomach, but it spewed forth. He arced it, trying to get some on the Forsaken, but Kirkus moved lithely out of the way, similar to Akio. Despite some of the best efforts of baby Cory, Akio had never gotten puke on him.

Terry's shoulders ached as he'd been thrown backward by the Forsaken's power. Terry struggled to get his feet back under him, but his stomach muscles protested, suggesting that he should stay doubled over. He ignored their protests and forced himself upright, managing a smile along with it.

"Is that all you got, little man?" Terry taunted.

"As you wish," Kirkus replied.

Terry was in the middle of saying "Touché" when the next blow landed. Two minutes later, Terry's shoulder had popped back out of the socket and he hung like a limp rag, sweat running from him in small streams.

Kirkus left the room, leaving the door open and the lights

on. It was the next step in getting Terry Henry Walton to watch the corridor in anticipation of pain.

It might take a while for Terry to fixate on the anticipation, but Kirkus didn't care. He had time. Kirkus's was the superior mind and with that, the entire world was his laboratory in which to work.

A shadow darkened the doorway as the servant entered, carrying a tray of food and a pitcher of water.

❖ ❖ ❖

BEIJING

Akio set the pod for maximum acceleration. He steeled himself against the forces imparted on his body as the ship raced from China back to Japan. The short trip ended with the pod landing and Akio jogging impatiently from it.

Once in his command center, he engaged Eve to search for the aircraft. If the Forsaken had a pod, he expected he'd be able to find it because of its unique technological signature. He'd searched for such technology after Bethany Anne left, but that was long ago.

The worst case that kept coming to the fore of his mind was that someone had used the Queen Bitch's absence to their advantage, coming to Earth for whatever reasons drove them.

He sat on his meditation pillow while Eve and the computers worked. He needed to clear the pre-conceived notions from his mind so they didn't distract him from the mission at hand. First order of business was to find Terry Henry Walton. Second, collect Char and the others. Third, ruin someone's day, but they should have expected that by taking the one man who strove to bring humanity back to civilization.

Akio wondered if the lost pod had been recovered. They'd looked for it after the events with the Sacred Clan, but it had never materialized. Akio hadn't thought about that missing pod in over fifty years.

"There are two blimps in the skies over Europe," Eve reported emotionlessly. "One over China and one outside the city of New York."

Akio didn't respond. Yuko sat patiently, waiting for the information that Akio was looking for.

"Eve. Factor in the notification from the Forsaken for the last raid. Analyze how the information came to us and use that as a base signature. That was a diversion to get me out of the way for their main effort, which was to seize Terry Henry. I am convinced of it. The Forsaken are rebuilding a global network," Akio stated, speaking slowly as he thought through the implication of his words.

That meant communications. China was in touch with someone else. If they were in the area, then the long flight over or around Japan would have been obvious to the satellites that Akio could access.

It was taking time, and Akio knew that the longer it took, the colder the trail would become.

He opened his eyes and activated his communication device. Cordelia answered immediately. "We are searching for your father with all the resources at our disposal. We will dispatch the pods shortly so we are in position *when* we find him," Akio explained.

"Hell hath no fury, Akio. My mother is ready to shake down every city from here to kingdom come, if need be, but that would not be best. The Forsaken have no idea what they've done," Cory firmly stated. "We'll be ready when you arrive."

Akio thought about telling her he'd call when the pods took off, but he saved his words. He knew what the pack and the members of the FDG were doing. Telling them when he'd arrive would change nothing. They would sit, and the wound would fester.

Their only relief would come when they faced their enemies. When they stared their fears down and let the courage of their convictions give them strength. It was what Terry preached day in, day out.

It was the very best of civilization, but to rescue him would bring out the worst in mankind. Akio heard it in Cory's voice.

Unbridled rage.

❖ ❖ ❖

CHICAGO

Char remained in human form to run alongside Joseph. In her Were form, she would have been faster, but getting there ahead of the Forsaken would not benefit her. She wanted him in the fight against the other Forsaken. He'd helped many times in the past twenty-five years.

She thought about Paris, but only for a moment. Joseph had saved the FDG from walking into an ambush. He'd finally earned her trust.

Char was asking for his help because she knew that she couldn't do it alone. If Akio never showed up, then she would have to continue on her current course, which meant that she needed every asset at her command.

She needed Joseph's abilities to help her understand the mind of the Forsaken that would do something so extreme as kidnapping Terry Henry. Minions had been sacrificed in the effort.

She would leave no door unopened and no room unchecked in her search for her husband.

Joseph's eyes clouded as he thought of what it must be like to have the love of such a woman. He clamped his jaws tightly and continued to push his body for more speed as they ran toward North Chicago.

"What do you need from me?" Joseph stammered as he tried to keep pace.

"All the insight you can bring, Joseph. You have the ability to read minds. That is a gift. We can use that and any influence you might be able to wield within a Forsaken stronghold. Make them hesitate, if only for a moment. I don't want them to kill TH when they realize that they've lost," Char shared sincerely.

"You know that I will do everything in my power to help free your husband and bring him home."

Joseph retreated within his own mind and concentrated on running. He could plan nothing, only hope that he was up for the challenge when it arose.

◆ ◆ ◆

NORTH CHICAGO

Mark walked up to Cory as she stood in front of the mayor's building.

"I'm sorry, Cory, that this happened to your father. I'm here for you. Anything you need. The colonel saved my life, helped me become a person I'm proud to see in the mirror." Mark hesitated, turning back to catch sight of the platoon double-timing their way through the park. "We're ready to go get him."

"Akio isn't on his way yet, but said he'd be coming soon," she told him without looking at the older man.

The company of warriors slowed to a walk. Blackie bellowed the cadence. They fell in step, halting on the single command. They remained in formation while Blackbeard checked in with the captain.

"We have some time. Get chow for those who haven't eaten. You know what it's like killing Forsaken on an empty stomach," Mark said with Terry-Henry-style bravado.

Blackbeard snickered. He returned to the company. "Listen up. We have a few minutes, so stack weapons. I'll stand guard. All the rest of you sorry asses, go get chow. Be back in thirty minutes, not one second longer!" he yelled.

At the mention of food, they almost lost all discipline, but the platoon sergeants started to yell. Felicity winced, as she always did at the brute force the FDG sometimes applied to its own people. But they came to attention, were released by their platoon sergeants, and like a mob, they ran for Claire's Diner.

Geronimo was standing to the side. He'd left the FDG after tweaking his knee. He couldn't run at the level the FDG demanded, and although Terry Henry had given him the opportunity to stay in a logistics role, he turned him down. It was combat or the quiet life of a rancher.

He joined his wife in taking care of the horses and the children. They had seven kids ranging from ten to twenty-four. The oldest was a member of the Force and had run off without saying anything to her father. He expected no less, because the lieutenant had told them there was hot chow on the objective.

Gerry laughed to himself. They always said there'd be hot chow on the objective, but there never was. It didn't matter. They accomplished the mission and didn't wait around. Other people filled the void after the FDG cut the head off whatever snake was terrorizing the populace.

Gerry leaned on his cane as he slowly approached. Mark smiled broadly and closed the distance, offering his hand.

The two friends shook warmly.

"What's going on?" Gerry wondered.

"The short version? Forsaken have kidnapped the colonel and we're waiting on Akio, because we're going after him."

"How did that happen?" Gerry was all ears.

Mark shrugged. "He killed eight of them, but they had an airship of some sort and flew away. Akio is going to take us to them so we can kill all the rest of them. If they've hurt the colonel, I suspect the major will lay waste to every fiber of their beings."

"I expect that she will. Give me a pistol, because I'm going, too," Gerry demanded.

Mark looked at his friend before shaking his head. "Can't do it, man. Only the active members of the Force," Mark said sadly.

The sound of a vehicle approaching drew their attention. It was one of the jeeps that they'd started to produce in one of the nearby factories that had been refurbished and restarted. It belched black smoke as it kicked up dirt during a high-speed cornering maneuver. The engine screamed as the driver revved the engine, powering through the curve and sliding to a stop next to the weapons stack.

Blevin was laughing as he climbed out, shuffling to the other side to help Corporal Heitz.

"Is this where they're boarding the train?" Blevin called.

"If they're going, I'm going," Gerry said flatly.

"They're not going," Mark said definitively as he intercepted the oldsters.

CHAPTER SEVEN

NORTH CHICAGO

Ted woke with a start, feeling refreshed but realizing he may have missed the pod.

"Oh, no!" Ted cried, getting up and high-stepping over the sleeping wolves. "Come on, my pretties!"

He usually wouldn't waste a brain cell thinking about going to war, but this was different. Someone had come into their house and taken the patriarch right out from under their noses. There was a line that one didn't cross, and that was it. Ted's peace and security had been shattered. His ability to work without interruption was gone as long as he was afraid that strangers could enter their town with impunity.

That wasn't the deal. The FDG was there to keep the bad out. Ted needed them to keep it out.

He'd been able to concentrate in peace since setting up in New Chicago. Terry Henry Walton and Charumati, the pack's alphas, saw to his safety and their security.

Although Ted lost his way briefly, getting sucked into the Mini Cooper and the allure of the wolf pack sleeping in the morning sun, he felt that he had to take things into his own hands to ensure status quo was regained. That meant finding and recovering Terry Henry Walton.

As in all things, Ted believed that if they wanted something done right, Ted had to be the one to do it.

Which meant that his equilibrium was in jeopardy if they left without him. He cursed himself for not seeing it sooner. He took his clothes off and changed into Were form.

He ran like the wind, the wolves barely able to keep up.

When they arrived, they found Cory and a few others still waiting. Ted changed into human form.

"Thank God you haven't left!" he exclaimed.

"Uncle Ted," Cory said softly, looking over his head. "Where are your clothes?"

He shrugged as if that was inconsequential. Felicity was enjoying the show, not in a hurry to see Ted get dressed. Billy shook his head and cackled.

"I don't mind you looking at the menu, my love," he told her before he started coughing. It had been getting worse of late.

He covered his mouth with his arm as the violence of his fit wracked his body. When he finished and pulled his arm away, the blood splatters stood out in sharp contrast to his pale skin. Billy looked at them oddly, something that shouldn't be there but was.

"That ain't good," Billy Spires suggested slowly in his gruff voice.

❖ ❖ ❖

Terry woke up with a start. It had not been a nightmare.

He was still in chains. TH stood on his toes and worked his shoulder until the nanocytes helped pop it back into place. He grunted with the effort.

Terry had no idea how long he'd been there. Hours? Days? His insides still felt like mush, which made him think that he'd only been out for a few minutes. He hated not knowing.

A shadow darkened the doorway. He flinched, which made him angry. Flinching was caused by fear. Was Terry Henry that afraid of the pain?

"FUCK YOU!" Terry screamed, straining at his shackles as he leaned forward to glare at the Forsaken.

But Kirkus wasn't the one who walked through the door. The Weretiger walked through, in human form, wearing slipper-like shoes and dressed casually in blue jeans and a floppy sweatshirt.

She looked at him, seemed to study him. She called into the hallway in Chinese. The other woman appeared with yet another tray of food. Terry could have eaten a whole buffalo, so he looked at the tray in anticipation. His mouth started to water.

The Weretiger held up a hand, stopping the servant.

Terry growled. He was being played. From pain to pleasure, to withholding pleasure, creating a different mental anguish.

"You will not hurt my servant?" the tall woman said with a Chinese accent. She articulated her words smoothly, as if she had spent a great deal of time in America.

"No. I did not before and I won't now. I will not because she is an innocent. Not so much for you, though," Terry cautioned, glaring at the Weretiger as he flexed his injured shoulder, willing the strength to return to it.

She signaled for her servant to feed the prisoner.

"Maybe we do as we are ordered. Not everyone is the great Terry Henry Walton, master of the world's destiny with final say over life and death itself," she said in a sultry voice.

Terry wondered if her accent and breathy voice were part of a ploy to get inside his mind, try to seduce him, but he had more control than that. Her body language suggested otherwise, so he discounted his initial impression.

"Master of life and death? Is that how you see me?" Terry asked between bites.

"It is what you do, is it not, keep the world safe from people like him, people like me?" she clarified.

"Not people like you. My wife is Were. You should see my daughter's ears. Wolf ears on a human. It could be her best feature, definitely makes her stand out," Terry said, smiling as he thought about Cory. "No, not Weres, but Forsaken. They have no place here, and even then, there is a Forsaken who I call a friend. Tell me, why did Kirkus come after me?"

She waited while Terry took a long drink from the pitcher. When it was drained, the servant wiped Terry's mouth, bowed to her mistress, and left.

"We know about Joseph," she answered softly.

"Then you know that I don't kill every Forsaken I meet. I don't kill every Were. Look at who is around me—Werewolves, Weretiger, and a Werebear. We have an elephant, but she's a real elephant, not Were. Can you imagine a Were elephant?" Terry continued to watch her closely, looking for any sign of duplicity, but he didn't see any twitches in her lips or eyes. "What's your name?"

Leaning against the wall, she blinked slowly without

replying. Terry waited. She pushed away from the wall, turned toward the door, and with one last glance in his direction, she was gone.

"Well now, whoever you are, what's your game? Or are you out there, Kirky-poo, listening in, doing your Forsaken voyeur thing? Well, you can suck my hairy balls. NO! Scratch that. I don't want your lips anywhere near there, so how about suck my ass or maybe you can just fuck off, you jack wagon."

Terry was feeling better by the minute. They'd fueled his body well. That meant round two of pain was coming. He didn't let that bother him. For the moment, he was good enough.

❖ ❖ ❖

Char and Joseph ran through the gate and continued running to Mayor's Park, where they found the weapons stacked and Cory talking with some of the others. She wondered why Ted was naked, but only for a moment.

"Akio should be on his way any time now," Cory reported as she handed the communication device back to her mother. Char looked at the small piece of technology.

Everyone used to carry something like that. Char kept hers for months after the fall before realizing that it was a waste, a relic. She didn't need anything on the phone to survive, which was what her life had devolved into.

She had hidden the phone in a sturdy building outside Toronto, refusing to simply throw it away as the others had.

Someday, she thought she would go back and get it. Charge it and see if there was anything from her former life that mattered.

Cory cocked her head as she looked at her mother. The

young woman's hairy, wolf ears stuck out beyond her hair.

Seeing Cordelia, Char knew that she didn't need any reminders from her past. It was a brand new world, a good place that they'd created from the ashes of humanity's conflagration.

She reached out to play with her daughter's ears as she stuffed the communication device into her pocket.

"Mom!" Cory pulled away and straightened her hair to drape it over her ear. Char laughed.

"The little things that make us all unique," she said, looking around her at the assembled group. Ted, Joseph, Billy, Felicity, Gerry, Mark, and a few others. "Ted. Go get some clothes on. What are those reprobates doing here?"

She smiled at the two old men as they waved, grinning.

"We're bringing the firepower, ma'am!" Blevin belted out, almost falling over as he snapped to attention and saluted. Heitz caught him but lost his grip on his cane. Mark stepped in to keep them both from falling. Gerry limped over to help.

"Is that still bothering you?" Cory asked, upset that he had refused her help. "Are you here because you want to go?"

Gerry nodded sheepishly.

"Pull up your pant leg," she ordered, passing Ted, who had not yet left. She turned to Ted. "And you, go get some clothes on!"

Gerry tugged at his pants, Mark helping to steady him. Cory gripped the man's knee and closed her eyes as she let her nanocytes flow through her hands. She squeezed his knee tightly to stay in contact as long as possible. Without linking to her flesh, the nanocytes quickly died. She stood up after a minute, weaving a little, dazed for a moment as she always was after healing someone.

Geronimo smirked as he flexed his knee. "Why didn't we

do this ages ago?" he asked.

"If your knee was good, what would you have done?" Cory asked sagely.

"I would still be a warrior in the Force!" he exclaimed proudly, before his exuberance faded.

"Because you needed to be with Kiwi and your family," Cory replied. The older men shifted uncomfortably. No one wanted to think they were being manipulated. Cory saw them all as family, but her father's demands on those in the Force de Guerre were monumental.

"It is my gift to use as I choose. No one has the right to demand that I use it on them. It is not theirs to command. We live in a society of free will, don't we? My father taught us that," Cory said passionately. She looked intently at the oldsters.

"We owe each other the gift of courtesy and honesty. If anyone is down, someone will always show up to help. It's what we do. If someone is where they shouldn't be, isn't it incumbent upon us to let them know? Kiwi was carrying a heavy burden, and you weren't there, but we were." Cory stopped to lift Gerry's chin to look at her. "Not helping you was my way of helping you. You didn't know that you need-ed that help, but you did. And look how it turned out. Your daughter is in the Force and doing well. Your family is happy. Kiwi is happy. I'd like to think that you are, too."

Gerry looked befuddled. He hadn't complained about his knee, only looked longingly at a life of adventure and excite-ment.

"I guess I was always a family man," he finally admitted. "The horses, Kiwi, the children, the tribe. My family."

"Who in the fuck started a shmoopfest?" Char yelled. "Family is why we're here because my husband is in the hands of some fucking Forsaken who's written his own fucking death certificate!"

Ted finally ran toward the housing units where they all still lived from when they'd first arrived. Felicity watched him go, the wolf pack running alongside. Despite Ted's foibles, he was a good-looking man, something he never paid any attention to.

The others sobered.

"Prop me up so I can fire my baby!" Corporal Heitz called. Blevin wasn't sure, but Char nodded. The two old men climbed back into the jeep, where Max stood in the saddle, bracing the fifty cal against his shoulder. He leaned backward and cocked the weapon, not an easy task even for a young man.

Shocked expressions preceded people diving out of the way. Even Billy ran two steps to the side and dove to the ground. That made him cough and hack again. Felicity joined him, to help him up.

"Get that idiot away from that gun!" the mayor yelled. Corporal Heitz bristled, but he immediately unloaded the weapon, and then refed the belt into it, before leaning back.

"I'm nobody's idiot," Max said coldly. Felicity was angry because Billy continued to cough, sending blood specks over his arm.

Cory joined the mayor, shaking her head sadly. Billy's problems were internal, where her nanocytes couldn't reach, unlike repairing a knee where she could get close enough to the damaged tissue.

They propped Billy up. Felicity looked daggers at the two oldsters and started to go after them. Char stopped her.

"They didn't do this. No one did," Char whispered,

looking deep into Felicity's eyes. "Seeing people grow old is the bane of our existence."

Felicity looked down, sighing heavily. Billy's skin was pale and clammy, his lips blue.

A somber mood descended on the group. Char and Cory stood together, looking more like sisters than mother and daughter. Char needed the anger. She wanted to tear into the Forsaken, into the minions, and rip Terry Henry from their grip.

"We will rise to the occasion, dear lady," Joseph told her.

CHAPTER EIGHT

"What kind of damn Neanderthals are you?" Mayra yelled from the kitchen as nearly one hundred members of the Force de Guerre stormed through the serving line.

Everyone tried to talk at the same time while cleaning out all the pans in rapid succession.

Mayra rallied the kitchen crew while those with empty trays waited impatiently.

"Now tell old Mayra why you're causing such a ruckus," the older woman demanded. Once again, they all started talking. She stopped them by holding up her hand. She heard the retiree table laughing. Mrs. Grimes was pushing ninety years old, but she still had plenty of fire. Claire Weathers had passed on not long after her husband passed away, but in her honor, they kept the name of the diner the same.

Margie Rose sat next to Mrs. Grimes and giggled. Both of

them raised their wooden spoons in solidarity with Mayra, who was soon to join them at the retiree table, where the two old women sat like mobsters from the before time.

The company calmed down. Margie Rose pointed her spoon at the mob. One person stepped up as the designated spokesman.

"Colonel Walton has been kidnapped, and we're waiting for our ride to go get him. We need energy, woman!" the young man shouted.

Someone punched him in the back of the head, almost knocking him down.

Another spoke. "We only have fifteen minutes to eat before we have to leave. Anything you can do would be greatly appreciated." It was Kiwi and Geronimo's young daughter who had stepped up. She wasn't the youngest in the company, but close.

"I should have simply asked you since I know you have manners, Ayashe." Mayra smiled. Someone pushed the private, and she stumbled. She turned and dove at the man, winding up to punch his face.

"No fighting!" Mayra said without raising her voice, but everyone heard. Ayashe stopped mid-swing.

Margie Rose and Mrs. Grimes banged their spoons on the table instead of clapping.

"Get that food out here. It's so they can rescue Terry Henry!" Mayra bellowed.

Most of the kitchen staff was comprised of the girls who Terry Henry had rescued twenty-six years earlier. She and her people had worked the fields until Margie Rose asked if she wanted to run the diner. It wasn't easy work and it wasn't women's work. That wasn't it at all.

It took a family to do it right, and that was what Claire

had originally built, and it seemed only natural that Mayra take over. Some of the girls never came out of the shells that the evil ones had put them into.

Terry and the FDG had killed those men, maybe too swiftly for some of the women and girls to gain closure. Mayra kept them close and together, showed them love and helped them feel safe. The FDG had done their share as well to protect the women rescued from that compound so long ago.

The food started arriving, much of it raw vegetables and smoked meats. They still hadn't been able to raise chickens in a way that provided eggs and meat for the thousands of people who lived in North Chicago. The herd of cattle made up for it. The Weathers legacy lived on as the oldest children were the tycoons of the cattle ranch.

The warriors moved quickly through the line, and soon everyone was eating. The only sounds were utensils ringing against the metal trays. They had nicer plates, pottery style that had been manufactured nearby, but the warriors preferred the trays, a holdover from the oldest members of the group.

They felt more in touch with the militaries of old.

The new people had no idea, having only heard the stories of those who lived in the before time. They accepted it without question.

"Join us, dear," old Mrs. Grimes said slowly and softly. Ayashe heard her and picked up her tray while still chewing, walking quickly to the retiree's table. She sat down and nodded to the old women.

"Reminds me of my cousin, John. He always ate so fast, just like that young pup Terry Henry Walton and your dad, Geronimo. Kiwi tried to slow him down, but he was too busy. They were all so busy," Mrs. Grimes lamented, looking through old gray eyes at a point on the ceiling. She sat in her wheelchair, barely able to stand on her own, let alone walk.

"John always told people that you don't mess with his cousin. He wasn't talking about me, because nobody messed with me, as a cousin by marriage. You see, my husband was a bit older than me." The old lady stopped as she teared up. She wiped her nose on a napkin before continuing.

"My man didn't survive the fall. He died protecting me. That is a Grimes trait. Selfless men doing what they have to for their family. No, John was talking about Cheryl Lynn, who needed his help. Her husband was bad news, but she had wonderful children." Mrs. Grimes looked into the distance, reliving those memories from long ago.

"John used to say that everyone was his friend until he pulled out a grenade. Then, they'd all disappear. He thought it was funny, but I can't imagine what he'd be doing with grenades. One day, he left with Bethany Anne and never came back. That one had a temper, she did, but only if you deserved it. She took care of my cousin, took care of Cheryl Lynn. I hope she's still taking care of John. He'd be old now." The old woman drifted off. She tried to grip her cup of tea, but her hand failed her, so she left the mug on the table.

Margie Rose leaned close and with one skeletal hand, wrapped in skin peppered with age spots, she patted the other, even thinner wrist. Mrs. Grimes seemed to be skin wrapped tightly over bones, with little muscle remaining. She'd always been thin, but the twilight of her life left her with little except her memories and those she would call friend.

Ayashe wasn't sure what to say. "I hope we all do Bethany Anne proud," she finally offered. "She'll be back, and we need to have the world in good order. There is so much work left to do, and it starts with getting the colonel back. I'm not sure what the Force would do without him. We can't look ourselves in the mirror thinking we left him behind."

Ayashe was only repeating what she'd heard the others say. Only Terry and Akio had ever met the legend that was Bethany Anne. Ayashe had no idea who she was or where she'd gone. The FDG had faith, because the colonel had faith.

Margie Rose's eyes glistened as she thought about the day she met Terry Henry. He needed a drink of water, and she gave it to him. His kindness was never in doubt. She remembered the years with Terry and Char living under her roof, in separate rooms and then together, inseparable ever since.

And they always treated her well.

"You find him, and you bring him home. I don't want to live in a world without Terry Henry Walton," she said selfishly. Her hand shook as she finished her tea. The first members of the Force delivered their trays to the scullery and hurried out. The current crew washing dishes was only on for the day, and then it would rotate to a different group. Everyone served their time in the diner. Thousands ate three meals a day in there every single day.

The diner was a respite from the outside world where hard work was the order of the day.

For the FDG, it was a break from making war. Margie Rose's lip curled at the thought of someone coming into their town and seizing TH. "Go now, dear, and you kill those bastards who had anything to do with this. Bring Terry home to us."

"I will, Margie Rose. Good day to you, and you too, Mrs. Grimes. I need to go. We'll do everything we can to make them pay," Ayashe promised.

❖ ❖ ❖

TERRY'S PRISON

"Look at you, player!" Terry called to a Forsaken he hadn't seen before. "Darkening my doorway at this late hour."

Terry had no idea what hour it was, which meant the Forsaken knew that he didn't know. The awareness ruined what TH was going for. "So what brings you to my neck of the woods, Mr. Sucky McSuckface?"

The Forsaken cocked an eyebrow. "Terry Henry, shame on you. Such violent thoughts raging through your mind," the young-looking man said.

"Why do you all have to be such twits? Well-spoken twits, mind you, but twits nonetheless." Terry worked his shoulders and flexed his stomach muscles as he prepared to tighten them to lessen the impact of the inevitable blows that the creature would deliver.

"If you were nicer, someone we could work with, we'd probably let you go," the Forsaken said smoothly, letting the words roll off his tongue as if trying to sell Terry a new product.

"When monkeys fly out of my ass!" Terry blurted. He let his mind drift to Lake Michigan and sailing, completely submersing himself in the wind and the sea as he tried to block the Forsaken's mind.

The Vampire edged closer. Terry closed his eyes, hearing the snap of the sail and thumping of small waves against the hull. He adjusted the tiller, trimming closer to the wind.

The impact surprised him as the Forsaken drove a fist into his mid-section. Terry jumped upward, pulling on his chains as he wrapped his legs around his tormentor.

The Forsaken's eyes shot wide in fear. Terry drove his forehead into the bridge of the creature's nose again and again. Terry's stomach muscles protested as he kept his enemy tightly in his grip.

The colonel leaned as far sideways as he could manage, trying to knock the Forsaken off its feet. He turned the other way, and the creature lost his balance. Terry flipped him onto his head, then stomped on his neck.

The Forsaken was able to roll out of TH's reach.

Terry kicked furiously, trying to hook one of the creature's legs and drag him back within reach. Terry pulled on his chains, straining against them as he stretched his body. Nothing gave. He leaned back and relaxed, letting his complaining shoulder settle.

Kirkus appeared in the doorway.

"Another sacrifice for your entertainment?" Terry said between heavy breaths.

"Not quite. His job was to soften you up a little, but that can wait. I see you are making no progress on the eyebolts. Keep at it, TH. I'm sure you'll succeed if you just give it enough of your attention and strength," Kirkus laughed. He grabbed the creature on the floor and pulled him roughly to his feet.

Kirkus pushed the other into the hallway, shut off the light, and closed the door.

Terry blinked in the near absolute darkness. "Twit," he said with a grin as his stomach muscles protested the endless pummeling.

CHAPTER NINE

NORTH CHICAGO

Timmons pulled Sue aside. He hugged her fiercely as he shook his head. He hadn't found out anything about TH. No one had seen or heard a thing. The lack of information was as frustrating to him as it was to Char.

He continued to hold Sue tightly until she gently pushed him away.

"What gives?" she asked. They'd been together for a while. She loved it when he was affectionate, but usually, she knew why.

"I thought about how I'd feel if something happened to you, if someone took you, and no one saw anything. I'd want to kill someone, but the enemy wouldn't be there. I see the frustration on Char's face. I'd lose my mind," Timmons whispered.

"We went through that years ago, and you moved

mountains for me," Sue purred.

"It wasn't quite all that." He let the words drift away as his mind took him to their incursion into Toronto. He blinked rapidly to fight off the tears.

She looked at him as his eyes glistened.

"This has been the best twenty-five years of my life," he whispered.

❖ ❖ ❖

Gunny Lacy searched for her husband, trying not to look frantic while doing it.

No one had seen James. Someone needed to stay home with the children, and they flipped for it because neither wanted to leave the Force. Lacy won the toss, and she remained with the FDG.

Terry Henry Walton and Charumati had gone out of their way to help James to transition. He'd gotten depressed, but Aaron stepped up to help, and soon James was incorporated into the fledgling school system.

He taught the kids survival courses and enjoyed that greatly. It brought him out of his funk. And then they had two more kids.

Lacy was getting ready to pack it in and join James in retirement by moving north. Terry and Char told incredible stories about their time in Canada.

"One last run," Lacy told Mark as she joined him in front of the mayor's building. She shook her head.

"James?"

"Yup. Can't find him," she answered.

"We'll be home in time for dinner. He won't even know that you've gone," Mark suggested.

"He'll know. That's why we need to pack it in, Mark. I'm tired of leaving, but I believe in what we're doing. I mean, fanatically believe. Where would the world be without us saving the people so they can grow without being someone's servant?"

Mark shrugged. "The FDG needs to do this. It needs to grow and be the stabilizing force for the whole planet. That's a tall order for one hundred people. We need thousands, and we need to be stationed all over the world so we can more rapidly respond. Maybe we move the FDG headquarters to Japan where Akio maintains his command post."

"Sounds like you've been thinking a lot about it," Lacy said, looking at the captain.

"I sit alone in the armory an awful lot." Mark didn't expound on that. He was too old to start a family, but he wasn't too old to find someone to spend his later years with.

He'd always been kind to Mayra, and she reciprocated. He wondered if he could retire and join her in the diner.

"This one's different, isn't it, Mark?" Lacy asked, not using Mark's rank as she would have in front of others from the Force.

"What kind of enemy are we facing who can walk in here and take someone like the colonel? Sure, he killed a few of them, but fuck! And now they have him in their house. What the hell does that look like? Yeah, this one is way different. This could be the strongest enemy we've ever faced," Mark said in a low voice, looking around to make sure no one could hear him.

"And combined, we're the strongest they will have ever faced. We will erase their existence, make no mistake about that," Lacy promised.

NOMAD AVENGED

◈ ◈ ◈

Akio looked anxiously at the screen. Eve was sifting through the entire planet's worth of data. At least the timeframe was constrained to a smaller period.

Eve had found something, but she was having trouble tracking it because it looked and acted like a pod. Despite their boxy shape, they were naturally stealthy because they weren't based on human technology.

Yuko was interested in how Akio was holding up. Recent demands on him had been great, and although Akio would never show strain, she didn't want it to eat at him or affect his well-ordered mind.

The data ran across the screen in rivers, crystallizing when it saw a pattern and then moved on when it turned out to be nothing.

Two hours later and Akio was still waiting.

"I cannot wait any longer, Eve. You stay here and keep at it. Find me that pod. I'll take all three pods and go to North Chicago. May the winds of fortune carry you home." Akio bowed deeply to Yuko, who returned his gesture. He jogged to the pod, and moments later, the three took off, soundlessly racing skyward.

Akio instructed the pods to accelerate at their maximum rate. He was pressed tightly into his seat as the g-forces reached extreme levels. Akio grunted with his effort to fight the pressure. Soon enough, he was weightless as the ship transitioned through the edge of the atmosphere before starting its descent. Then Akio was pressed into his seat for another five minutes of spleen-crushing acceleration, followed by getting thrown forward for several minutes of chest-pounding deceleration.

One hour after taking off from Japan, Akio landed in North Chicago. He recovered from the effects of the g-forces almost instantly. He straightened the pistols set on his black uniform. He looked paramilitary, as he always did, ready to blend in with the dark recesses of any terrain.

His face was grim as the ramp lowered, and he stepped onto the grass of Mayor's Park.

◈ ◈ ◈

NORTH CHICAGO

Char was first to see the pods approach.

"About fucking time," she said to herself. Cory pursed her lips, having nothing to say, waiting for Akio to tell them where they were going.

Timmons had his arm wrapped around Sue's slender waist as they watched and waited.

Gene grumbled and rocked impatiently. Aaron stood close to him. The two had become fast friends over the years as the two who were both outsiders and insiders.

Ted held his wolf pack back. He wanted them to go but knew there wouldn't be room. He liked having his pack with them. They were the closest thing he had to a family.

The other Weres stood patiently. They'd been ready to go and were willing to wait a few more minutes. They knew what was on the other end. Battles with Forsaken meant pain. Someone always got hurt.

Clovis broke free and ran to the pod where the ramp was lowering and barked furiously while his tail wagged out of control.

The oldsters fired up the jeep and revved the engine, preparing to drive the vehicle into the pod. They'd taken one of the jeeps on an earlier mission, so they knew it would fit.

Kiwi arrived as the pods were descending and found her husband, where he showed that his knee was healed. She nodded tersely, having just found out about the colonel. She assumed that she'd be going, too. She demanded to go, but wasn't sure who to talk with.

With the company of warriors from the FDG, half the town, and only three pods, someone would have to stay behind.

Char looked at the determined faces surrounding her. She knew that Terry Henry was well-respected in North Chicago, but the highest honor one can pay is to risk their life for another. None of the people there were concerned about the danger. They knew that something had to be done.

And they all wanted a part of doing it.

Akio walked from the pod wearing his usual expression. He dipped his head in recognition of the large number of people in the welcoming party. He expected no less for Terry Henry Walton, but he was at a loss as to how they were going to accommodate all the volunteers.

The big coonhound pup came close, barking and dipping into play pose, prancing and barking some more. Akio sent a sense of calm to the dog. Clovis relaxed and joined Akio at his side, where the shorter man could easily scratch behind the dog's ears.

He waved for Char to join him. Since Cory wasn't going to leave her mother's side, she came too. Char held up a hand to prevent a mob from approaching.

"Charumati-san. Cordelia-san." Akio bowed thirty degrees to the two women. They bowed in return. "Before you ask, we have not located him yet. Please, follow me."

Without a word, they walked onto the shuttle. He stood before a computer screen that was linked through satellites to the system that Eve was operating. The EI was focusing on the eastern half of what used to be the United States.

A voice came over the pod's sound system. "I think we have them," Eve said with a tinge of excitement.

They watched as Eve zoomed in on open fields off the southern end of Lake Michigan. A small shadow appeared, and after refocusing, the unmistakable shape of a pod filled the screen.

"Where did a Forsaken get a pod?" Char asked.

"That, I can't be sure of, but I think it was the pod that the Sacred Clan stole many, many years ago," Akio replied. "Eve. Can you track it?"

"Of course, Akio-san, now that I know what to look for, where to look for it, and when to look. I will piece it together frame by frame. It's flying low, so I suspect it did not go very much farther," Eve said before going silent.

The image remained on the screen while the EI worked her behind- the-scenes magic.

"I think we need to saddle up," Cory suggested. Char nodded and the two left the aircraft.

Char waved the leadership to her. The Were folk came without question. Mark brought the lieutenant, the company gunny, and the platoon sergeants. Blevin climbed out of the jeep and hurried to join the others. Gerry and Kiwi helped the old man and were the final ones to join the mix.

"You all know what will and won't fit. I'd love to take everyone, but they all can't go. The tac team goes, without a doubt. We are going up against Forsaken. How many? I have no idea. What kind of stronghold? No idea. How many human minions? No idea. You get the picture. Opinions, people," Char demanded. She gritted her teeth and pounded her fist into her hand. Every second was one more second that Terry Henry was captive.

She found the waiting unbearable.

"Then it's important that we go, bring the jeep with the ma deuce, grenades, and rocket launchers," Blevin suggested helpfully. "Just in case."

"More gear means fewer people," Char replied.

Mark shuffled his feet and shook his head. "We've gone up against Forsaken before. Only you guys have a real chance against them." Mark nodded toward the pack. "We'll handle the cannon fodder. We'll bring two platoons, and that should give us enough room. I think we'll need the jeep, assuming we don't have to land in the boonies somewhere. Are they coming?"

Everyone looked at Ted's wolf pack. He raised his eyebrows as he looked to Char for confirmation.

"Not this time, Ted. Sorry," Char apologized.

Cory put a hand on his shoulder to comfort him. He didn't usually like people touching his person, but he always welcomed Cordelia. Her touch brought him peace.

"They'll be fine staying here," Ted said firmly.

Char looked at the coonhound. "Don't even," Cory stated preemptively. Char rolled her eyes.

"Load the jeep, First Sergeant Blevin. Lacy and you two--" Char pointed to Gerry and Kiwi. "--go with them and ride in that pod. You all spread out."

The Weres nodded.

Timmons and Sue headed toward the second pod. Gene and Aaron remained with Char and Cory. Adams and Merrit joined the group manhandling the jeep into the third pod, which they called number three.

Shonna and Ted walked toward the second pod, joining Timmons and Sue.

The look on the faces of those who couldn't go ranged from anger to soul-crushing despair. Mark didn't budge. He sent the two platoons to fill in the spaces on the pods. He put the platoons that would remain behind on watch.

"If we don't return, who is going to protect these people?" Cory heard Mark say. The thought was sobering. The young woman never contemplated that they wouldn't come back.

She wondered why she had such complete faith in Akio. Maybe it was because Akio always brought them home. More likely it was because her father's loyalty to Akio was complete and unquestioning.

Cordelia trusted her father like he trusted Akio.

"Thank you, Akio," Cory told him when she took her seat. Akio nodded briefly before returning his attention to the screen where Eve was funneling the video composite she was building of the Forsaken's pod's flight profile.

Blackie stayed in pod three with the jeep and the heavy weapons. Those he hand-selected to operate the weapons were squeezed in around the jeep. Blevin and Heitz sat in the front seats of the vehicle, and both were smiling.

Mark got the thumbs up from Blackie and from the platoon sergeant in the second pod, Sergeant Allison. The captain signaled for pods two and three to button up. He ran up the ramp to the first pod and took his seat next to Joseph. Char acknowledged him before buttoning up the aircraft.

Akio ordered the pods airborne. They flew slowly away, staying low as they headed over the lake, toward the open water, and then turned south to pick up the trail where Eve first spotted the enemy pod.

"We will find them, Char-san," Akio promised as the pod picked up speed.

TERRY'S PRISON

"Ass-grabbing, ball-slapping shitbag!" Terry yelled when Kirkus walked through the door. Terry wasn't angry. He just wanted the Forsaken to get a clear delivery of what Terry really thought.

"Good morning to you, too, TH!" Kirkus said happily. "It's time that we celebrate your first week in your new home."

Terry was instantly confused. He flexed his stomach muscles and rotated his shoulder. Had he been there a week, certain injuries would have already healed. He couldn't believe that he'd been gone more than half a day, and he suspected it was less than that. He'd only eaten three times while in captivity.

No. Nice mind game, motherfucker. Can you hear me now, cheesedick? Terry thought.

Kirkus stopped approaching but continued to smile. He raised a hand and snapped his fingers. The Weretiger strolled in. She was in her human form and dressed the same as the first time Terry had seen her.

"Hi, kitten," he said in a friendly manner. He had no animosity for her. He wondered how Weretigers got along. Aaron had been alone for a long time. Would he be able to relate to another Weretiger or had the Werewolves and Werebear ruined him?

Terry chuckled thinking about it. He felt tired but was in good spirits.

"I have to say, TH, your once-disciplined mind so easily breaks down with a little pain and lack of real sleep. What you would give for a bed," the Forsaken taunted.

"Doesn't quite take a mind-reader to figure that one out, ass-face," Terry replied casually.

"Kick him in the balls," Kirkus ordered.

The Weretiger hesitated before taking two steps forward, spinning and driving her heel into Terry's pelvis, a couple inches from the directed target. Terry grunted and doubled over as much as he could while still chained to the walls.

He thought of his first mission to China with Akio. They'd gone deep into the mine. He'd been the weak link in the mission, the only one who couldn't see in the dark, but he'd gone in any way. Terry had been in danger too many times to feel fear like normal people. He had confidence in his own abilities and those who surrounded him.

His fear was of failure, failing the good people who put their faith in him. Char was brave and undyingly faithful. He knew that he was safe as anyone could be when he was with her. She was a fierce fighter. Now that Cory was grown, she'd redoubled her efforts to train and get better, be more deadly. He thought that she'd become the deadliest killer he'd ever met who wasn't like Akio or Bethany Anne.

Terry's lip curled of its own accord. He yanked on his chains, hoping to snap a link or a bolt. He only needed one arm free, and he'd finish the Forsaken.

Kirkus laughed. "I think you'll need more than one arm to deal with me, Colonel Terry Henry Walton. You think you can defeat me with one arm tied behind your back? Maybe we should try it and see." The Forsaken was no longer smiling.

The air in the room turned cold as the Forsaken contemplated Terry's punishment. Kirkus waved the Weretiger to the side as he stepped past her.

He dove in and punched Terry quickly, jabbing his ribs and hitting his face.

Terry lashed out with his legs, but the Forsaken blocked them. Kirkus rotated and with extra force, landed the heel of his hand on Terry's mouth, splitting his lips and loosening a tooth.

Kirkus stepped back as Terry reeled from the impact. He licked his lips, tasting the blood. "You could be the biggest jagoff I've ever met," Terry slurred as his mouth filled with blood. He spit it at the Forsaken, hoping the nanocytes would have pity and survive long enough outside his body to kill his enemy.

Kirkus laughed at him and with head raised, strutted from the room, leaving the light on, the door open, and the Weretiger behind.

"My name is Yanmei," she said softly, picking up a rag and approaching Terry. She didn't shy away from his unshackled legs. She didn't think that she had to.

She dabbed at his lips, then called for her servant. The petite woman appeared almost immediately carrying a pitcher of water. Yanmei took the pitcher and held it to Terry's lips. He winced at first contact but drank readily.

Once the pitcher was drained, Terry slowed his breathing, trying to relax and let the nanocytes do their thing.

The Weretiger watched him for a few moments and then left.

CHAPTER TEN

FLYING IN THE POD

Blackie sat next to the young Sergeant Nickles. "It took that pudknocker, General Tsao, five years before he raised his ugly head. We had to go in with the same kind of load out we got today," Blackie told him.

"Well before my time, Lieutenant," the sergeant replied. "That was twenty years ago."

The lieutenant recounted the story as they flew, delivering only the highlights.

Everyone was listening intently to the story. Some had been there, most had not. It had been a long time since the Force de Guerre had destroyed the army of General Tsao.

"Over a thousand soldiers walked down that road, one hundred and seventeen lived to see the sunrise. That's the story people need to know. Get on the wrong side of the new world, and the FDG is coming for you, coming to ruin your day. Fuck those guys," Blackie said without looking at anyone in the pod.

"To whoever took him? Fuck you! We're coming, and you ain't seen nothin' yet, bitches! Here's to Terry Henry Walton!" Corporal Max Heitz bellowed with renewed vigor.

"To Terry Henry Walton!" those in the pod echoed. Adams and Merrit nodded. They were ready to do their part. They were ready to take on the Forsaken who had come into their house in the middle of the night.

❖ ❖ ❖

TERRY'S PRISON

Terry stood upright, trying to relax. His legs didn't ache, which told him that he hadn't been there that long. His shoulder was healing, once again. The nanocytes had already knitted the skin of his lips back together and tightened his teeth. He worked his jaw, loosening it. He'd been clenching it ever since getting punched.

"Let me out of these chains, pus-wad and we'll see what you can do in a straight up fight. Jagoffs. All the Forsaken are jagoffs. Maybe it's in your nature or something. I don't know. Twits," Terry said, having a perfectly congenial conversation with himself. Since the lights were on, he took the opportunity to study the eyebolts.

He flexed and pulled, looking for the slightest movement. He continued working it. Terry was able to hold himself upright and brace his feet on the wall on one side to give himself additional leverage, but the bolt wouldn't move.

Terry had been chained into a corner, with his arms stretched to the side and slightly upward. The eyebolts were over his head, on each wall. He had limited movement, not enough to give it a good yank.

He let himself back down to the floor and found Yanmei leaning in the doorway watching.

"Hey!" he exclaimed with a scowl. "Don't you people ever knock?"

"I would think less of you if you weren't trying to escape," she offered.

"That might matter if I cared what you thought about me. If you release me, then I would care a whole lot," Terry replied with a half-smile. He saw that she had changed clothes again.

"Are you twins or something?" he asked.

"No, just one of me, but my room is not far. I prefer comfort; he prefers the elegant look."

Terry wondered why she was trying to become his friend. He wouldn't mention that it seemed forced. If he did, the Forsaken would be in her mind and see that she had failed. Terry held out hope that he could block the creature.

In the interim, he decided to play the game. The eyebolts weren't budging.

"I can't release you, because he wouldn't take it well," she finally answered. "Care for a game of chess?"

She produced a board from behind her back.

"I'm pretty busy," he started, smiling. She didn't see the humor in it. "Of course, I'd love to play. It's been awhile so you'll have to forgive me until I shake off some of the rust."

She set up the board on the floor in front of him. She sat cross-legged and arranged the pieces. "You are the guest. You shall play white."

He called out the square for his pawn. Yanmei moved it, and the battle began.

Yanmei was not a fast player, where Terry had been conditioned with timed play. He had never had time to contemplate moves and countermoves five plays ahead. He could usually think three moves ahead, and that had always been good enough.

The young-looking woman would make her play, and within seconds, Terry would move. She'd look at the board for several minutes before taking her next turn. What felt like forty-five minutes in and the game was barely underway. Terry took a risk and paid for it, losing a knight and a bishop in rapid succession. He slowed down, but the damage was done.

He started playing for a draw and succeeded, though he was unhappy that he forced himself into playing a defensive game, but sometimes, as in life, the best one could hope for was a draw.

She gathered the board and pieces, thanked him for the good game, and left.

"I'll be damned," he told himself when he was alone. "Pleasure and pain. Pain and pleasure. What is this fucker's game? Play away, Kirkus. I'll figure your ass out or die trying. You can take that to the bank!"

Terry was fiercely defiant. Then he realized that there were no banks. They were some of the first things to go after the fall. Food was useful. Money was not. Anything needed to get food was useful. That wasn't money. Tellers, managers, and security had simply walked away after the WWDE.

"Nice one, TH. You need some new idiomatic expressions. Maybe you should make your own," Terry told himself. He thought long and hard, but nothing came to him.

A shadow darkened the doorway, and his muscles tightened. It was Yanmei's servant with a tray of food and water.

He was angry at how he tensed. Kirkus had scored a point, and he wasn't even there.

"I could really use a beer if you have one," he said softly. She simply shook her head, not understanding what he was saying.

FLYING IN THE POD

Sue, Timmons, Shonna, and Ted sat together in the second pod. The warriors were packed in tightly around them. The space in the middle of the pod was empty. Timmons shook his head.

"What?" Sue asked.

"We could have brought some more weapons or more of something. It's wasted space. Terry would be mad," Timmons replied.

"He can be mad after we've saved him," Sue suggested.

Ayashe released her seatbelt and staggered across the pod to kneel in front of Sue and Timmons. They looked up together.

"You look worried," Kiwi and Gerry's daughter told them.

"We are always going into combat," Timmons dodged.

"No, you aren't," she replied.

"Too smart for your own good," Sue said, smiling. "This is different, for sure, because we don't have Terry Henry Walton leading us. There is no finer warrior. He takes no unnecessary risks. His battle plans are meant to minimize our casualties and maximize those of the enemy, while always accomplishing the mission. He is the consummate professional when it comes to war."

"And the major isn't?" Ayashe asked in a young voice.

"We will follow anywhere she leads, if that answers your question," Timmons answered.

"As would we." Ayashe looked at the perpetually-young faces of the Werewolves. They returned her gaze, waiting for the question they could see she wanted to ask. Her face turned troubled. "What do we do if something happens to the colonel?"

"We comfort ourselves that we did everything we could to prevent it, then we keep Char from burning the Earth. Her grief will be more than all the rest of ours combined. We help her, and then we move forward, keep civilization from collapsing under the weight of tyranny," Timmons said.

Sue looked at her mate, wondering where the philosophy had come from. Tyranny wasn't a word that Timmons used.

"If we don't move forward, then what would we do? Why would we exist?" Sue asked.

Ayashe shrugged.

"Why do you ask?" Timmons wondered.

"My mother saw Metaguas today. Someone is going to die. I know it. It's been a long time since the rabbit has appeared, but there he was, in the park with the rest of us. I didn't see anything, but my mother has the gift."

"Then we will see who Metaguas has come for. No matter what, the survivors will always carry on, because they have to. We have a responsibility to humanity. Our alpha has declared that as our purpose. It is how things are and how they will be," Sue replied matter-of-factly.

Timmons grabbed one of the young woman's shoulders and Sue took the other. "We're in this together. All of us. We'll see it to the end, won't we, Ayashe? No matter how it turns out, the one thing we guarantee is that we will win or die trying."

❖ ❖ ❖

"I gotta pee," Max told his friend.

"What the hell am I supposed to do about it?" Blevin replied. Someone nearby snickered.

"I don't know. Drop the ramp and let me pee out the back." Max started struggling to pull himself out of the jeep.

Adams and Merrit watched curiously, wondering what the oldster was going to do. They wondered what it was like to get old, something they wouldn't experience for a long time.

"Sit your ass down!" Blackbeard bellowed. Max gave him the finger.

The lieutenant calmly got up and climbed over people, balancing himself between the seats along the side of the pod and the jeep.

"Come on, Max. We're not dropping the ramp. You have to hold it," Blackie told the old man.

"Listen here, you little fucker, when you get to be my age, peeing isn't something you can turn on and off. When it's time, it's time. It's like when the rain comes. You can't hold that back. Now, I gotta go, Lieutenant. What are you going to do to accommodate the troops?"

Blackie rolled his eyes and shook his head.

"Who's got a mortar round?" A couple of the warriors raised their hands. He pointed to one of them. "Take the round out and give me the case."

There was some discombobulation as the warrior removed his pack and pulled the round out, holding it away from himself so he didn't dent the delicate fins.

Blackie took the case--a long, plastic cylinder sealed at one end with a cap at the other. The gasket was intact, which meant the case would seal after Max was done taking care of business.

"Here. Don't make a mess," Blackie tried to order.

"No guarantees, Lieutenant. Thanks, but I would have been perfectly happy hanging it off the end of the ramp!" Max and Blevin both laughed as they thought how that would have worked.

"Sure. Can you imagine the colonel's face when we told him we let you fall out the back of the pod?"

Max mumbled something, but he was already at work, taking care of his personal business. Blackie made a hasty retreat, giving the thumbs up to the warrior still holding the mortar round in his hands and a look of confusion on his face.

Blackie studiously ignored him as did the rest of the warriors. He resigned himself to holding the mortar round and remembered the old adage of "never volunteer for anything."

CHAPTER ELEVEN

FLYING IN THE POD

The pod slowed as Eve painstakingly reconstructed the other pod's path. The target had flown beneath the clouds, forcing Eve to search every opening on the original flight path, but the pod never reappeared. Then Eve traced the borders of the entire clouded area and searched, looking for where the pod emerged.

The clouds covered half a state. That was too much territory to search, but if Char was given no other choice, she would walk every inch of the ground.

From the southern end of what used to be Indiana to the southern border of Kentucky and for a similar distance from east to west was the refined search area.

"I am afraid, Charumati-san, that this is the best we can do. The Forsaken's pod has landed somewhere within this area." Akio drew a box with his hands over the map displayed on the screen.

NOMAD AVENGED

"What's the biggest city in that area?" Char asked.

"Louisville," Akio replied, clearly pronouncing the 's.'

"Let's start with Louisville," she suggested, pronouncing it as 'Looavull.' "We'll pass low and slow over the city, separate the pods by ten miles. If a Forsaken is down there, we'll sense him."

Akio nodded and quickly programmed the flight computers of the three aircraft.

They covered the distance quickly and slowed once they reached the outskirts of what had once been Louisville, Kentucky. The city had never recovered, but it looked like the small towns that cropped up on the outskirts were thriving. In an agricultural world, it made sense that places best suited for growing food would rebound the best.

The pods made three passes over the city, discovering three Werewolves, but no Forsaken.

"We'll come back later to find out who you are," she promised the unknown Weres on the ground. "Anything, Joseph?"

The Forsaken shook his head. "I share your concern," was all he said. He closed his eyes and leaned back, digging deeper into the etheric, continuing his own search for his brethren. They'd crossed the line, and he had no intention of protecting them.

He liked the status quo, where he could be himself and not worry about getting his head cut off. Twenty-five years ago, Joseph had excused himself from the community of North Chicago and gone to sleep. He woke four years later, refreshed and famished. Terry had welcomed him back like one would an old friend. Joseph didn't have to wonder. He knew.

Terry Henry Walton was his only friend. The others tolerated him, but given a choice, they wouldn't simply stand

114

around and do nothing with the Forsaken. Terry was special, because he would and he had no errant thoughts. He did it because he was a nice guy, not because he felt pity. Joseph would know that, and that wasn't Terry.

Joseph opened his eyes and found himself on the pod. The others were occupying their minds with a variety of diversions, many simply daydreaming. Char was singularly focused. Her aura glowed like the top of an erupting volcano. He was amazed that she wasn't tearing the inside of the pod apart in her furor.

The warriors had their eyes closed, most of them sleeping. Terry had taught them to sleep when they could because once they hit the ground, they never knew when they'd be able to rest.

Terry had learned the trick during his time in the Marine Corps. He learned the lesson well because Terry could fall asleep anywhere at a moment's notice and wake up thirty minutes later completely refreshed. Joseph was always amazed by the man's glowing red eyes. He'd achieved near Forsaken-level strength and speed. With his training, he was better than the Forsaken.

But not better than a dozen of them at one time. "We need to find him," Joseph blurted without thinking. He was afraid of what his fellows would do to the Terry Henry Walton.

"I couldn't agree more," Char replied, looking at the Forsaken through narrowed eyes, wondering what he'd been thinking about.

❖ ❖ ❖

Timmons and Sue held hands as the pod flew back and forth in the hopes that one of the Were folk would sense a Forsaken on the grounds below and that Akio or Joseph would be able to touch Terry's mind, know that he was alive.

From Louisville, they continued east to Frankfort and Lexington. They slowly crisscrossed the skies over the mostly abandoned cities and their growing suburbs. The world was starting to return. From dozens of people here and there to hundreds in the more fertile areas.

The mountains of Kentucky fought off the majority of the heat and desert that had swallowed most of North America. From west of the Appalachians to the Rockies, the land was arid. What used to be Oklahoma and Kansas was nothing but parched land.

Timmons had run the pack through Arizona and New Mexico, almost killing them in the heat and dry, but they made it and were stronger because of it.

They wouldn't do it again, not because they couldn't but because it sucked so badly.

Kentucky wasn't anything like that. It was green and growing. Water flowed in the rivers. Wildlife was extensive, and the people were almost as populous as what they found in Chicago or New York, even though they were spread farther apart.

"Maybe we can retire here?" Sue quipped.

"Retirement," Timmons said slowly. "What a concept. I wonder if we'll ever have anything like that, or if we'll be running that power plant, working, fighting evil until the day we die."

Sue shrugged. "That's a long ways off. I think we'll like getting old, unless this was the first shot in a war among those from the Unknown World."

Timmons had to think about that. He couldn't fathom being at war for the rest of his life. It would be like being condemned to Hell--fighting every day of their existence.

The speaker in the pod came to life.

"Attention all pods," Char announced. "Forsaken spotted south of Louisville. We're going in, triangular pattern. Special tac teams only converge on the target. He's alone and we need information. Force personnel, small arms only. Secure the pods and wait for our return."

Sue and Timmons's pod twisted mid-air and raced in a new direction. They sensed the Forsaken in the distance.

"Now we're getting somewhere," Sue said through gritted teeth.

❖ ❖ ❖

"Joseph, when we load back up, I think you should be in a different pod. Jump in number three. We can cover more territory that way. It's redundant having you and Akio on the same pod," Char said conversationally.

"Wow!" Joseph whispered. "You've raised me to Akio's level. I don't know what to say."

"Bullshit," Char shot back. "You always have something to say." She reached past Cory to punch the Forsaken in the chest, forcing herself to smile. The strain was taking its toll on her, creating wrinkles around her eyes. She tried to keep it light, but Terry's abduction was tearing her apart.

"How he in peace is wounded, not in war," Joseph quoted. "I believe you're a fan of Shakespeare?"

"Be great in act, as you have been in thought," Char replied before her face turned sour. The target Forsaken was not far. She looked at Akio across the pod, but his expression hadn't changed.

Joseph's face went blank as he reached out. His fellow Forsaken knew they were coming and had started to run. The pod jerked as it flew to cut him off. The other two pods responded instantly.

Their descent was rapid, and the ramp opened before they hit the ground. With Joseph and Akio, the Were folk bolted from the pod. From the two other pods, the rest of the pack hit the ground running.

Some changed into Were form; others didn't. Char never told them to change or not. The choice was theirs.

Gene removed his clothes as he ran off the pod, throwing them to the side and leaping from the ramp. His Werebear paws dug into the dirt and he raced past Char, Cory, and Clovis. The pup always kept up. He'd been brought up running after Cory and accepted it as a normal way to travel.

The warriors from the FDG filed off and took up positions fifty yards away in a circle around the pod as they defended their ride. They remained behind cover and watched impatiently, hoping for a quick resolution.

Joseph and Akio split up, each going in a different direction as they tried to bracket their target. Aaron kept pace with Char and Cory, remaining in human form. He'd never been able to remember what he did as a Weretiger, and that bothered him.

Aaron also considered himself to be Cory's protector. He'd been there almost every single day of her life. He'd been close with Kaeden and Kimber, having watched over them on numerous occasions while the Force deployed.

He'd been their teacher, taught them to read. He'd been their friend and to Kaeden, he'd been his savior, having pulled him from the water and the wreckage. Aaron felt the sting of the jagged cut he'd gotten during that effort. It quickly healed completely, but he could still feel it. After that, he'd changed into his Were form and didn't remember a thing until he changed back.

Aaron thought that both Kae and Kim liked him as a tiger. They said so, when he was in human form. He wished he'd remembered the fun they said they had together.

He stayed close to Cory, ready to change to a Weretiger should she be threatened. The ever-vigilant Charumati was leading the way, determined to find her husband, and Aaron didn't think she'd let anyone get past her.

There was no doubt who was in charge. Even Akio was in a supporting role to the purple-eyed Werewolf.

The Forsaken stopped running.

"It knows we're here," Char told the others as she maintained her blistering pace. Gene loped ahead, not overexerting himself. He slavered as if a good meal waited. Usually he wasn't a drooler, but even he wanted this over with and his body was anxious.

They all hoped that this Forsaken would bring them one step closer to Terry Henry Walton.

The middle-aged looking man was backed against a tree, staying in the shade. He was completely covered and looked uncomfortable. Akio and Joseph stood nearby. The three Were teams arrived at the same time. Sue and Timmons remained in the woods behind the Forsaken while Shonna, Merrit, and Ted stayed in the clearing. They made way for Char, Cory, Aaron, and Gene.

Cordelia tried to walk alongside her mother, but Char put out an arm and forced her daughter to walk behind, bracketed by the Weretiger and the Werebear. Clovis growled and barked at the Forsaken.

Nothing was as deadly as a cornered animal.

"Where is he?" Char asked, dispensing with the usual verbal jousting that Forsaken seemed to prefer and that TH reveled in.

"I'm sure I don't know," the Forsaken replied. Char looked to Akio. He nodded almost imperceptibly. Joseph held up a hand and approached.

"Why would you say such a thing, when you know we can tell you're lying?" Joseph asked, cocking his head so the other could see his face under the wide brim of his leather hat.

"If you know it isn't true, then it's not a lie," the Forsaken stated casually. He wore a sword and had a rifle slung over his shoulder, but his arms were crossed and his hands empty. He stood defiant but not aggressive.

"Where are the other Forsaken? Where did they take Terry Henry Walton?" Char demanded.

The Forsaken's mind clamped shut, and Akio drew his sword.

CHAPTER TWELVE

TERRY'S PRISON

"Tell me, TH, why do you insist on sacrificing yourself for the weak?" Kirkus pressed.

"For the seventy-fourth time, it's the right thing to do. None of my previous answers convinced you?" Terry replied, looking into the Forsaken's eyes and seeing nothing except a dark cruelty. Terry was obligated to add a taunt. "You warthog-faced buffoon. You are dense as a post."

Kirkus didn't acknowledge that he'd heard Terry speak.

"Moral compass? Because of your moral compass. Let's review, shall we," Kirkus started in a low voice as he sought to make his point. "You return home to find your wife and daughter dead after a valiant battle. You *killed the murderer*, but then you went on to kill everyone else who was present. The images of their deaths, TH? Even *I* find those shocking."

It had been nearly fifty years since that happened, yet it had stamped darkness onto his soul. He knew that he'd be capable of that again if anyone put him in the same situation. His moral compass pointed true unless someone came after his family.

He was ready to become Hell on Earth. All he needed was to be tipped over the edge. Kirkus laughed.

"Payback? I am making amends for the last time I willingly left my family when I shouldn't have to work for someone who saw me as a warm body and not a man with a family. This is my chance to fix that." Terry knew there was no reason to lie, so he embraced his honesty, something the Forsaken probably found uncomfortable.

"I will share that they have come for you. They are fumbling around, flying in circles nowhere near here. We've tossed out a bit of bait to keep them distracted while we return to your little home. Kimber, Kaeden, and you have grandchildren, too! Can you imagine William and Mary Ellen playing in the hallways here?" Kirkus smiled, but it wasn't of happiness or even forced to get a rise from TH. It was a smile of pure evil.

"Because *I* can see it, Terry Henry," Kirkus added.

Terry froze, glaring at the creature that called itself Kirkus. He lived underground because daylight was death. Terry had been taken while it was still dark. He wondered who was going to North Chicago.

Char would not have left the community unprotected. Kimber and Kaeden were no pushovers either, assuming they stayed behind. Kae still carried the knife that Terry had given a boy of nine. Kimber was a martial arts master. Cory was almost as good as her mother, almost as fast.

And there was the FDG. His captain, lieutenant, and sergeants wouldn't let anything happen to the civilians. They'd lay down their lives to protect them.

It wasn't just Terry's moral compass that the Forsaken was questioning. It was all of theirs.

Terry smiled. The Forsaken was challenging humanity's right to exist as free and independent souls. They would refuse. All of them. Forsaken running rampant around the community? They'd have to fight them all. Everyone would swing a shovel or a chair, stab with a knife.

Everyone was armed with at least a knife. Terry had encouraged it, made sure that the residents had something with which to defend themselves. He wanted to join the fight, take it to the Forsaken right there.

Terry ground his teeth together, clenching so tightly that his jaw started to ache. He opened his mouth and took deep breaths, calming himself. The only way to help his family was to escape his chains, something he'd done emotionally, a long time ago, when he returned to mankind.

"We will wipe you and your spawn from the face of the Earth," Terry promised, pulling and twisting on his all-too-real chains.

❖ ❖ ❖

NORTH CHICAGO

Kimberly and Kaeden had wanted to go, but Char had put her foot down. They were to stay and watch over the grandchildren.

As well as the others.

Jim stood nearby, older, still a large man, but his running days were well behind him. He helped Mark on occasion, but he preferred working in the kitchen, probably because he loved to eat. Without the running, he was starting to fill out.

Jim patted his ample stomach and found a seat on the steps.

The pods were not long gone, but those standing around watched the sky as if their return was imminent.

The two sergeants who had been left behind had dispatched their platoons to key areas around North Chicago.

No warrior stood post alone. Two full squads surrounded the mayor's building, walking the perimeter with weapons at the ready.

Billy was back in his chair, looking pale as he took rapid, shallow breaths.

"I remember a long time ago when my security chief manned a security patrol at our house," Billy managed to say between gasping breaths.

"And they tried to build that god-awful thing in our front yard, Billy dear," Felicity drawled. "I know what you did for me. You made me out to be the bad guy!"

Her laugh was musical, but Billy's degenerated into a racking cough. "Don't make me laugh, woman," he mumbled after the latest fit, but he was smiling.

"But Marcus hadn't been after us. He was after Terry and Char. This time? No different. There's always someone coming after them. Can't people leave good folks like them alone? We've known those two for a long time, almost thirty years, and they've never been anything but selfless. That attracts the wrong sort, I guess," Felicity said, squeezing Billy's hand tightly.

"I guess," he croaked.

"Kim. Kae. What's next?" Felicity was curious. Usually, Terry Henry and Char did what they needed to do, keeping the mayor informed with what she needed to know, but they weren't there to tell her.

Kim shrugged. Kae looked at the mayor. "We guard and we wait. They will return and when they do, they'll have our father with them, because Mother would not leave him behind. If the pods return without him, Mother will not be on board, because they will have had to kill her. I guarantee you that."

"Sergeant Boris!" Kim called as she walked toward one of the uniformed warriors. "What is your load out?"

"Standard loads, five point five six millimeter, full-metal jacket," he replied, cocking his head at the question.

"I recommend you give your people some of the silver-tipped ammo, at least the first one or two in each magazine." She wasn't a tall woman, but her demeanor made her seem larger. She spoke confidently and had a way about her that people noticed. When she talked, people listened.

Sergeant Boris nodded and passed the word. The two newest recruits left their posts and ran at top speed toward the barracks and the weapons locker where the special ammunition was stored.

They had fallen out with silver-tipped rounds, but those who were selected to remain behind had given theirs to the warriors who were going. Boris wasn't sure how many of the special rounds were left, but as long as the number was greater than zero, he wanted them.

The other platoon sergeant, Sergeant Allen, had his people farther out, creating a secondary line of defense. Anyone coming from the outside would be dealt with first by his platoon before encountering the close-in defense.

Two platoons weren't enough to protect all of North Chicago. They had to spread themselves thin.

Maybe *too* thin.

NOMAD AVENGED

❖ ❖ ❖

The Forsaken had clammed up, not saying a word, not thinking a thought that Akio or Joseph could hear, not giving anything away.

Char moved in close using a fighter's stance, ready for the Forsaken to lash out. He was a daywalker, weaker than those who had to stay in the dark.

Joseph moved close on one side, and Akio, the other.

"Tell me, you motherfucker!" Char growled. Like a whisper of the wind, her fist flew at the Forsaken's face. He caught it in his hand, smiling.

A sunbeam through the branches flashed off Akio's blade as he swung and sliced through the Vampire's arm. The Forsaken howled, grabbing his stump with his free hand. Char reared back and drove her fist home, splattering the Forsaken's nose. He tried to run, but Joseph caught him, hiked him over his hip, and body-slammed him into the tree trunk.

Joseph jumped back as Akio's blade arced a second time and removed the Forsaken's other arm. The creature howled as dark blood spurted, then slowed. It continued to ebb with the beating of the Forsaken's heart.

"The Black Knight's had worse," Timmons quipped. Sue stifled a laugh before elbowing her mate in the ribs.

Cory had no idea what they meant and was miffed at the horseplay. Char was too hell-bent on getting answers, but she expected that she'd find it funny later, when TH was safe. All of that passed through her mind in a millisecond. She returned to the business at hand, grabbing the Forsaken by his shirt, hauling him to his feet, and slamming him against the tree.

"I think the lady asked you a question, brother," Joseph said softly. The Forsaken snapped his head to the side to glare at his fellow Forsaken.

"How could you?" the Forsaken grunted.

"Winners." Joseph waved his open hand at everyone who wasn't bleeding, and then he pointed at the armless Forsaken. "Losers."

The Forsaken lunged at Joseph, but Char caught him and slammed him back into the tree. "You know where he is. Terry Henry Walton and the scum who took him. Tell me," she demanded.

Akio caressed the creature's face with his katana, then let it hover in front of its throat. He started to saw with only the slightest pressure. The razor sharp blade sliced neatly into the skin.

"If you cut my throat, I won't be able to tell you where he is…" Before the Forsaken finished speaking, Akio thrust forward and drew the blade backwards, pressing toward the tree and cleanly removing the creature's head from its body.

Char looked furiously at Akio, clenching and unclenching her hands compulsively. Joseph put a hand on her shoulder. She whipped around to face him.

"We need to go," Joseph said. "They're holding him in Mammoth Cave."

"Run like the wind!" Char yelled, turned, and ran. Clovis was barking furiously at the dead body, watching it shrivel as its nanocytes died.

"Come on, you dumb dog," Cory said, swatting his hindquarters and getting him to run with her. The others were already on their way out of the clearing, fleeing toward their respective pods. Joseph joined Adams and Merrit as they headed for pod three.

Cory ran for all she was worth, but Char was outdistancing her. Aaron was up ahead but slowed to let her catch up. Together, they pounded through the grassy underbrush of a gently rolling hill. When they came upon the pod, Char was waving at them impatiently. As soon as their feet and paws hit the ramp, it started to close.

❖ ❖ ❖

MAMMOTH CAVE

Kirkus looked at his minions, still angry that Terry Henry had killed so many of his best foot soldiers. Those that remained were not the cream of the crop, so he was stuck adding the human slaves to the mix. He expected that the humans would die in the attack, but they would distract whoever was left long enough for his Forsaken minions to do their work, capture Walton's children and bring them back.

Kirkus didn't care if they recovered any of the humans or not. Once Kirkus was the power, people would flock to him. They would be easy to manipulate and he'd have an army in no time. General Gilbert Kirkus, master of the world.

He liked it, but back to the business at hand.

The humans he was sending were eager, having been properly brainwashed, but he'd always intended them to be food.

"Your mission is to wreak havoc among anyone who is not the child or grandchild of Terry Henry and Charumati Walton," he informed them.

One brave human raised his hand. "How do we know them?" he asked.

Kirkus rolled his eyes. "Because they'll tell you." He

pointed at the Forsaken looking down on the human minions.

The man nodded happily.

Twelve humans and four Forsaken stood in the gaping maw that was the entrance to Mammoth Cave. An earthquake sometime around the fall had widened the opening and made it possible for the Forsaken to move a stolen pod in.

Under the cover of darkness, he'd flown it from the hangar in rural Virginia throughout the eastern seaboard and the Appalachians, looking for the perfect place to hide and start building an empire.

When he came across Mammoth Cave, he knew he had found the right spot.

Kirkus had established security, buttoned the pod up tightly, and gone to sleep. For decades he slept, rising thirty years after the WWDE. That was when he started to build. He became the denizen of the night, scouring everything that remained to find the technology he needed to access the satellites he knew were still in orbit.

Satellites that the Queen Bitch had used to command. He had no doubt he could get into them. He had a pod, the technology that it contained, and his own immense intellect. He refused to consider that he wouldn't be able to do it.

He knew about the satellites because he'd once been close enough to find out, learn what there was to know about the Kurtherians and the technology they'd left on Earth. Mr. Smith had recognized his potential and helped him to expand his mind in the short time they had together.

It was enough.

Once Kirkus had tapped into the satellites, he had to build his database from scratch, learn how the world had changed since the world's worst day ever.

In time, he started making short forays into the populated areas, taking the pod and landing silently in the dark of night. He learned of the FDG and the colonel who ran it with his purple-eyed partner, a beautiful woman with a silver streak of hair running down one side of her face.

Kirkus knew that they were enhanced. He didn't know to what degree, only that they were different, more like him than normal humans.

The Forsaken learned how different when he took the pod on a well-planned raid to capture Terry Henry Walton and his partner.

Kirkus reached out and grabbed one of the other Forsaken. "How did he kill eight of you?" he demanded. It wasn't the first time he'd asked that question.

"He was faster, deadlier. His eyes glowed red, but he's not like us. I've never seen anything like it." The Forsaken cowered before Kirkus.

"Of course *you've* never seen anything like him. *No one has seen anything like that, you moron!*" Kirkus sent the minion sprawling. The lesser Forsaken hurried to get up and brush himself off, glaring at the humans, but they were looking down. They knew not to incur Kirkus's wrath.

"Go, you fucking toads, and bring me back those kids!" Kirkus screamed maniacally before storming away.

CHAPTER THIRTEEN

Mammoth Cave had been a massive national park back in the day. Now, it was heavily overgrown, and the entrance wasn't as obvious as Char had hoped. The whole world looked different, but the interstates and main roads still held much of the vegetation at bay.

Akio had found the old interstate and followed it. They missed the turn off for the park and had to circle back. The second and third pods took up a position in the general area and hovered while Akio searched.

The minutes stretched as the pod slowed to a crawl, looking for a winding road that was no longer there.

Eve's voice projected through the pod's sound system. "A pod has just appeared and is now flying north. I've input the coordinates from where it came. You can be there in moments. Would you like me to send the other pods after this new one?"

Char's mind raced, and her decision was quick.

"Send the pod number two after them at best possible speed. Get close enough so our people can sense who is on board. The rest of us are going spelunking."

Akio issued the orders, and two pods raced for the spot from where the other pod had appeared.

"Put me on speaker with pod two, please," she asked Akio.

He nodded to her. "Timmons! Take charge and hunt those bastards down, wherever they are going. Keep us informed," she said loudly, looking out the window as the pod descended toward a massive cave mouth.

"Will do, Char," Timmons replied. He had nothing else to say. Everyone in the second pod was pressed heavily into the seats as the pod continued its acceleration in an attempt to overtake the intruder.

"And if possible, take that pod away from them. We could use a new piece of gear. Do us proud, Sergeant Allison," Char told them.

"Always," the sergeant replied.

❖ ❖ ❖

"What do you mean they were right there?" Kirkus bellowed toward the communications station.

A voice crackled through the speaker. "When we emerged from the cave mouth, three pods were scattered across the area. We headed north, and one pod is following. I lost the other two. I think they stayed there. I'm sorry, but they had to see where we came from."

Kirkus fumed. He picked up a cup and threw it, shattering it on the far wall of the cave.

He was left with nearly no manpower, only the weakest of

servants, a Weretiger, and his wits.

Kirkus had never been one to count on winging it. He had built booby traps into the cave and knew it was time to activate them. The Forsaken walked through in his mind how the events would unfold. Terry's people would land and enter the cave, they'd be worn down by traps of various types, and then Kirkus would kill them one by one.

No one could stand up to him.

"Carry out your mission. When the other pod lands, kill everyone on it and take it. We could use another one of those," Kirkus replied calmly and then put the microphone back in its cradle.

He looked up for a moment and then ran for the cave mouth. There was much work to do.

❖ ❖ ❖

FLYING IN THE POD

Timmons and the others hung on as the pod executed a series of high-speed maneuvers. According to the screen, the other pod was headed straight for Chicago, by which Timmons assumed that it was headed for North Chicago. They'd taken all the comm devices. He had no way to warn them.

"We need to fix that," Timmons said.

Sergeant Allison glanced his way.

"Comm. We need more comm devices," Timmons explained. Sue squeezed his leg as the adrenaline started to course through her body.

The pod leapt forward. "Forsaken," Sue said loudly. "Four and twelve humans."

Allison looked at her. "Four Forsaken and twelve humans?" he asked.

The Werewolves nodded in unison. Shonna and Ted had sensed them, too.

"Listen up!" the sergeant belted out. "There are twelve humans on that pod. They are our business. We cannot let them gain a foothold in North Chicago. No matter where they land, we will put ourselves between them and the community. This time, we're not looking to take any prisoners. There are four others on that pod. Forsaken. Our friends here will take care of them, but if you get a shot, you all have silver-tipped bullets. Use them wisely."

Allison looked from one to the next, insisting on the thumbs up sign to show that they understood.

The pod dipped and jerked as they flew between some of the tall buildings still standing in old Chicago.

"Why are we doing this, Eve? Can't we just fly above it all?" Timmons asked the ceiling.

Eve's disembodied voice replied, "Of course." And the ship headed upward, greatly smoothing the ride as they kept the other pod in sight. Eve took the pod higher.

Soon the other pod exited the winding confines of the remnants of Chicago's skyscrapers and launched itself due north. Timmons followed its line of travel on the projected map.

"We're going home, people. Try not to shoot any of our own," he cautioned, gritting his teeth.

The sanctuary of North Chicago was about to be invaded for the second time that day. And he couldn't have that. "NO MERCY!" he yelled.

Sue jumped at the outburst.

A chorus of oorahs filled the inside of the pod. The FDG

warriors performed one final check of their weapons, that their helmet chinstraps were tight, and that their flak vests were closed. With one hand on their rifles and the second hand on their restraints, they prepared to disembark.

Their pod followed the other in.

❖ ❖ ❖

MAMMOTH CAVE ENTRANCE

Akio hovered the pod outside the entrance, hesitant to enter. "It is too confined within," he said in a tone that wasn't open for discussion. "We need to find a place to land and then enter the cave on foot."

"Lower the ramp," Char growled, looking through narrowed eyes at the video projection of the cave's entrance. "I'll jump down."

Akio hesitated. He zoomed out to find a landing spot only a hundred yards away, but it was only big enough for one pod at a time.

"New plan, Char-san," Akio said as he fingered one of the two pistols at his side. "We will descend close to the mouth. We will jump into the entrance and then the pod will land. The others will disembark and move here. Our pod will return to hover over the entrance. The number three pod will then land and disembark. We will have three groups. Not optimal, but it will suffice. I can only sense one Forsaken within the cave and nothing else. There is too much rock. We will know more once we are inside."

Char nodded tersely as she stood and walked to the ramp. She relayed the plan to the pod three, ordering the jeep to remain in the clearing with the pods to protect them. She'd seen that there was no way they could get inside the cave. People would be hard-pressed to get through the entrance, but it was perfectly suited for a craft like a pod.

Akio wouldn't risk taking a pod inside. It was the enemy's stronghold, and this was shaping up to be the final battle.

◈ ◈ ◈

TERRY'S PRISON

Yanmei hurried down the corridor. Terry heard her coming, which was out of the norm. She had foregone stealth for speed.

That meant something was happening.

She entered Terry's prison and shut the door behind her. She leaned her back against the wall beside it and waited.

"That's different," Terry said conversationally. He watched to see what else her body language would give away. She didn't reply to his statement, so he took a more direct route.

"What's happening?" he asked.

"I am to watch you, and if necessary, I am to kill you." She talked without changing her facial expression. The rest of her body was stiff, as if made of wood.

At least she hadn't changed into her Were form.

"So there is something happening. Why didn't Kirkus come? Isn't he all about domination and control?" Terry probed.

She blinked, but made no move to answer. Yanmei leaned over and put an ear to the door, then shrugged almost imperceptibly and resumed her position against the wall.

"Did you bring your chess board?" Terry wondered, knowing that she hadn't.

She held out two empty hands.

"I'm sorry, too. I won't make the same mistake I made in the last game," he promised with a smile. "Since it looks like we're going to be here for some uncertain amount of time, do you mind if I tell you a story?"

Yanmei looked at him, blinking slowly, expression unchanged.

"Cory was five years old, and everything in North Chicago was going great. Everyone had enough to eat. The power was on, and we were expanding the operational grid. Even as far out as the Weathers' ranch, we had electric lights. We decided it was time for a little camping trip. Just me, Char, and our daughter Cory. We also adopted two kids that we found wandering the Wastelands, Kim and Kae. We took four horses and headed north toward Canada. We spent two weeks getting there because we weren't in a hurry. It was an opportunity for Char and me to teach them some life skills, living off the land, that kind of stuff. We had a good life in North Chicago, and things were coming pretty easy. The kids went to school, and the adults went to work. Everyone ate in Claire's Diner."

Terry shifted his feet and rolled his shoulders as much as he could. He needed to let his arms hang at his sides, at least long enough to let the blood flow back into his fingers. He flexed his hands and tried to encourage the nanocytes to stretch their legs. His stomach started to feel better.

Yanmei watched him emotionlessly.

"You know what we found in Canada?"

Terry waited, but there was no answer.

"Peace. We found peace. A small cabin on a lake where the fish were always biting. Game that wasn't afraid of humans. We stayed there for a week, then two weeks. It was like our own paradise. Char and I talked about staying. The FDG had competent leadership, so they didn't need me."

Terry hopped from one foot to the other as he encouraged blood flow. He expected that he'd take a beating soon and needed his body to be ready.

"But then we got a call from Akio. Do you know who he is? He's one of the Queen's Bitches, left behind when she went to space. She's out there somewhere, protecting the world that tried to kill itself. Ain't that some shit?" Terry looked at a spot on the wall and shook his head. Someone like the Queen risking their life for a belief that humanity deserved to be saved.

And humanity turned the world into a shithole. Terry had a hard time reconciling himself with what they found in the Wasteland. Humanity had tried to kill the planet, and Mother Earth was still reeling from the body blows. But she'd survived. Humanity had survived. Maybe the Queen's faith wasn't misplaced.

At least it wasn't when it came to her faith in TH and Akio.

"Akio is here to help us save what's left and rebuild. Anyway, he had a mission that only the great Terry Henry Walton could perform. Terry Henry and his partner, the Werewolf Charumati," Terry said, tossing his head and smirking at the sound of his name coming from his own lips.

"You wouldn't believe how much I love her. It physically hurts me to be apart from her. We've been together for something like twenty-nine years. *Hear my soul speak. Of the very instant that I saw you, did my heart fly at your service*, Shakespeare said in *The Tempest*. There were no truer words written. Or maybe, *Love looks not with the eyes, but with the mind, and therefore is winged Cupid blind*. Although she's really something to look at, too. I'm pretty sure that I've never seen a more beautiful woman, no disrespect intended toward you. I see her looking over her shoulder at me, purple eyes glowing, and mischief in her face. CHAR!" Terry yelled all of a sudden, grimacing.

His body convulsed as he flexed his muscles, enraged at still being chained to the wall.

"Akio called and told us he was on his way to North Chicago to pick us up, along with Char's pack. But we were in Canada, far to the north. He adjusted his flight and came to Canada. We had to leave the horses behind, and we had kids with us, but none of that mattered. The world needed to be saved. We flew to New York City, a place that Akio seems to have a hard-on for, as we keep going back there to make sure they are on the straight and narrow."

Terry shifted his shoulders again, leaning one way until the chain would give no more, then leaning the opposite direction.

"Is there any way you could loosen this chain just a touch?" he asked. She ran her tongue over her lips to moisten them. Terry was thirsty, too. He wondered when he'd next get a drink.

He had remembered a classified terrorist threat briefing he'd once prepared regarding Brigadier General Dozier and his kidnapping by the Red Brigade in Italy. He'd avoided talking about religion and politics, but instead talked about those things where they had common ground. The terrorists started to see him as a human being and not as a prisoner in their silent war. The general's guard, who was supposed to kill him in case of a rescue attempt, did not, and the general was freed and the entire cell captured without the special police force firing a shot.

"In New York City, we found a small group trying to act like a gang. Char, Kim, Kae, and I left the pod. Cory was with Akio. I thought it odd that he didn't go, but he's Akio and had his reasons. We confronted the gang. We let them encircle us because we wanted them in one place, you know, so we could talk with them all at one time. A couple thought Kimber would make a nice addition to their group. You should have seen her beat the crap out of those two knuckleheads. Once we showed them the error of their ways, which earned their leader two broken arms, they were much more amenable to a humane approach to rebuilding society."

Terry watched the Weretiger's reactions to see if he was having an impact, becoming a real person in her mind, but she gave nothing away.

"Cory healed the man. Five-years-old and she didn't want to see him in pain. That made him a believer. The New Yorkers wouldn't have stood a chance. Kim and Kae could have taken that whole gang by themselves. They learned at a young age that there's nothing like being able to protect yourself. That gang leader? I think he's the mayor of one of the biggest boroughs in New York. Last time there, we found them making it into a real city again. They have power, food, and even trade. In another fifty years, I think we may see New York City at the heart of a modern world. I'd like to be around to see that, visit there with my kids and their kids. And my wife, too. God, I miss her," Terry lamented, eyes tearing, but he blinked them away.

He could smell a fight coming and needed to be out of his chains.

"Do you have anyone?" Terry asked softly.

CHAPTER FOURTEEN

MAMMOTH CAVE ENTRANCE

The ramp descended, and Char didn't hesitate as she ran off the back and jumped. The two-story drop was through light branches. Char kept her legs together on her way down, one hand clasped over her face. She hit the ground hard, but let her knees collapse as she pushed, rolling on the ground and coming up ready to fight. Akio was right behind her, then Gene, who was less graceful, crashed through the branches and hit the ground with a heavy thud. Aaron landed on a higher branch and bounced down the tree like an elf, landing lightly next to Gene, who he helped to his feet.

Gene angrily ripped his clothes off and changed into Were form. Aaron thought about changing and decided he needed to be at the top of his game. He looked sad as he became a Weretiger because he knew that he would remember nothing of what happened from this point until he changed back.

Joseph hit the ground and crumpled into a pile. His combat roll left a lot to be desired.

Another grunt drew their attention as Cory hit and rolled. She came to her feet and quickly brushed herself off. Char glared at her and Cory glared back, putting her hands on her hips for added emphasis. "Stay behind me," Char conceded.

Akio drew his pistols and walked quickly toward the cave. The others fell in behind him.

At one time, the cave mouth had concrete steps leading down to an area called Houchins Narrows, a wide and high tunnel that led downward into the main part of the cave. That was before the fall. Afterward, the quake had opened things up, while also destroying the visitor's entrance. It was now covered in boulders of all sizes, making for a rough climb to get past.

Cool air breezed past as they worked their way through the jumble at the entrance.

Akio stopped every few steps to look and sniff. He continued through the rubble at the entrance until he was first to the bottom, where Houchins Narrows spread out before him. This was the pod's hangar, judging from the cleared space and netting on the cave's roof to catch rocks before they fell on the aircraft.

Char stopped when she heard a noise behind her. Mark was waving with the warriors from the first pod. She cupped her hands around her mouth. "Follow us in. Third pod cover the entrance. Be ready to shoot that pod down if it comes back and tries to enter the cave."

Mark gave the thumbs up and started sending the two squads down, one man at a time. They dislodged rocks and stumbled as they hurried to catch up.

Cory was the last one of the first group. She turned and

glared at the squad leader. "Slow down and get yourself under control!" she snarled. He recoiled as if slapped. Cory was usually calm, the one every one looked to for keeping the peace.

She put a finger to her lips and he passed it up the line. Be quiet.

Akio raised a fist to hold the others in place as he remained still and studied every detail of the cave from near to far, low to high. Char froze while standing on the final rock before setting foot on the tunnel floor. The stone below the fall remained smooth from hundreds of thousands of feet walking over it, millions of gallons of water polishing it.

Akio took one careful step forward and then another. On his third step, he dodged as a massive explosion rocked the cave wall, sending debris flying across the path he was on.

Char was hit and rolled to the side. She was able to get her hands up, blocking her face with her pistols. Char let the force of the blast carry her before hitting and rolling into a ball, to minimize the beating.

Gene was behind her. The smaller rocks hit and bounced off the Werebear. He shook the dust off and roared his anger.

The Weretiger leapt the rocks and snarled as cats do, screaming as the dust settled. Cory jumped from rock to rock to get past Gene, but he held her up, blocking her way as he forced a path through the newly fallen rock. Joseph remained behind Cory.

Char was already getting up, cuts marked her arms from the chips that had sprayed across her, but she hadn't been on the receiving end of the bone-crushing boulders like Akio had been. She worked her way through the fallen rocks, pistols out and ready, watching the tunnel carefully, wondering when and from where the next strike would happen.

She reached Akio, his body shattered, but he was still alive and already healing. His lightning quick dodge had saved his life, a maneuver that only one of his ability could have pulled off.

She cleared the rocks away and helped him to sit. He gurgled and wheezed with each breath. "I still live," he whispered.

"For a long time to come, my friend," Char replied softly, letting him rest his head against her hand. Cory finally appeared at Char's side.

She started to put her hands on Akio's chest, but Char stopped her. "He has his own nanocytes. They may fight against yours," Char tried to explain.

"Then I'll stop. Mother, please, let me do what I do," Cory pleaded. Char removed her hand and nodded once.

Clovis tried to stuff his dog nose in between Cory and Akio, but Char pulled the big pup back.

Cory looked more closely at Akio, trying to determine which wounds were the worst. His arms and legs were battered, but the crushed rib cage and torn up lungs needed her attention the most. Her first impression had been right.

She spread her fingers as she gently worked her hands beneath Akio's combat shirt. His body trembled at the touch, but only slightly. He was fighting to control the pain. Akio was attempting to meditate, free his mind and body to quicken the healing process.

Cory shuddered as her nanocytes started to interact with Akio's. A spasm torqued her abdomen and she lurched forward. Char grabbed her by the arms, ready to pull her away.

"It's okay," Cory gasped, visibly relaxing as each moment passed. A slight blue glow emanated from beneath Akio's shirt as his chest filled out, repairing itself at a fantastic pace.

Cordelia sighed heavily and fell backward.

Char caught her and gently leaned her next to Akio. Cory was breathing slowly and rhythmically. Her hands continued to glow for a few more seconds before the light faded. Her eyelids fluttered as she struggled to wake up. When she forced her eyes open, they glowed blue.

"Are you okay?" Char wondered, not seeing anything unusual besides her daughter's eyes.

"I am. Tired, but getting over that quickly. What?" Cory asked.

"Your eyes. They're glowing," Char said matter-of-factly as she kept stealing glances down the tunnel. "We need to go. You should stay here with Akio."

"No," Cory replied. She stood, took two deep breaths, and motioned for her mother to precede her.

Gene was fifty yards down the tunnel, turning his head back and forth as if one ear would hear better than the other. The Weretiger was standing between Cory and where the booby trap had been detonated. Joseph was standing next to Aaron, studying the cavern wall.

"What if there are more of those things?" Char asked Cory.

"Then you'll need me more than ever," Cory answered, gesturing impatiently down the tunnel.

"Leave one person with Akio and follow us," Char ordered the captain.

Mark looked at Ayashe and motioned for her to remain.

"No way," she argued. Mark almost came unglued.

"You'll do as you're ordered, Private!" he barked, before turning to follow the Were folk and the Forsaken into the cave. Ayashe stood in front of Akio and watched her fellow warriors enter the cave.

She wasn't one for being insubordinate, but she realized what made her speak out of turn.

Ayashe was afraid. She was alone in the enemy's stronghold, and she was afraid.

"Nothing to fear, Ayashe-chan," Akio said softly from behind her. She jumped and then hung her head as she worked through the irrationality of it all.

"Yes, Master Akio," she replied respectfully.

"Come, sit with me." Akio patted the rock next to him, grimacing with the effort.

Who was she to turn him down? She joined him, sitting up and watching down the tunnel, her finger outside of the trigger guard and her thumb on the selector lever, ready to flip it off safe.

◈ ◈ ◈

TERRY'S PRISON

The thunder of the explosion reverberated through the walls of Terry's room. He could feel the vibration through the chains and into his arms. He smiled.

"They're here, aren't they?" he asked.

Yanmei licked her lips as she started to breathe faster, more the trait of a cat trapped where it didn't want to be than a human waiting for orders from her master.

"Let me go and we'll leave here together. We'll protect each other and then, when we're back with Char and the pack, we'll protect you from him. We'll protect the whole world from him, but you have to let me go first," Terry told her in a gentle voice as he tried to sound rational, logical, when what he really wanted to do was scream in fury.

Char was close, and someone was blowing stuff up. He hoped the explosion was from breaching charges. He couldn't tell. C4 sounded like HMX sounded like TATP through the bedrock beyond the walls.

It told him that he was in a cave. More importantly, it told him that he'd been found.

Yanmei knew it, and she was starting to feel the strain. Her once stoic features were starting to twitch.

"You can't protect me from him. You can't even protect yourself," she blurted, smirking and waving a hand to take in a chained Terry Henry.

"Do you know how many of them came after me?" he asked coldly. She didn't respond. "A dozen of them. Eight didn't come back. I'm giving you my word that if you let me out of here, I will die to protect you, just like I would anyone facing an evil like Kirkus."

She licked her lips again and chanced a look at the door. She reached for the knob, but it was already turning.

◆ ◆ ◆

FLYING IN THE POD

Timmons, Sue, and Sergeant Allison had their eyes glued to the screen as the other pod slowed on approach to the former naval base that the community of New Boulder had taken over and claimed as North Chicago.

The pod flew low over the FDG barracks and the diner. It headed for Mayor's Park, where it hovered for an instant and then dropped to the deck with the back ramp lowering as it landed.

"Hurry!" Allison yelled, and the pod lurched and pitched

nose first as it rapidly closed the distance between it and the other pod.

❖ ❖ ❖

NORTH CHICAGO

"Hey! They're back already!" one of the Force privates yelled. "Pass it on!"

He slung his rifle over his shoulder as he left his post and walked toward the rapidly descending pod. He wondered why they were coming in so quickly, as well as a second pod, too.

Somebody's injured. They need help, he thought and started to run. He pulled up short when he saw within the pod. Men and Forsaken. He didn't recognize them.

"IT'S A TRAP!" he yelled as an Uzi burped and the bullets hit his vest and climbed upward, tearing into his neck and face. He flopped to the ground in a fountain of blood.

Boris took a knee and with his first two shots, dropped the first two humans off the pod. The others ran free and scattered. He flipped his selector switch to a three-round burst and sprayed the running men. The Forsaken walked off last.

Boris thumbed the magazine release and the magazine fell free. He slapped in the magazine with the silver bullets on top, pulled the charging handle, and sent an unfired round flying. He let the handle go to ram the first silver-tipped round into the chamber, and Boris took aim.

The Forsaken stepped from the pod and looked right at the sergeant. Boris's mind filled with overwhelming terror. He dropped his weapon, covered his ears, and ran.

The Forsaken laughed. He looked at the other residents. Two of the minions were running toward the entrance to a building that overlooked the landing field. A young woman was trying to drag an old man inside while a young man and young woman looked on defiantly. A third young woman put her hand on the young man's arm, joining him in glaring at the new arrivals.

"That's them!" the Forsaken yelled, pointing to the people at the entrance of the large brick building.

Two of the minions broke into a full sprint, expecting their targets to run. They didn't. Kaeden and Kimber stood their ground. As the two men vaulted up the steps, they were met by snap-kicks. They fell in unison. Kae throat-punched his and rolled him to the side. Kim kicked her opponent twice more until he stilled, then she stomped on his neck. The snap of a bone breaking echoed from the walls behind them.

Kae and Kim descended to the sidewalk and assumed their fighting positions. They didn't have firearms while the enemy did, but they heard the Forsaken's call. The enemy had come for them, and they weren't going to be taken.

Kimber vowed never to be taken again, not alive anyway.

A second pod approached rapidly, flaring to land. The rear deck dropped and friendly faces bellowed their war cries as they ran into Mayor's Park.

CHAPTER FIFTEEN

TERRY'S PRISON

Yanmei jumped back but quickly relaxed. Terry stared wide-eyed as the knob turned and the door slowly opened. Yanmei's servant sheepishly entered and closed the door behind her.

Terry's first thought was about food and water, and she had brought nothing with her. He was disappointed, his hunger and thirst at the forefront of his mind.

That made him feel bad, because he could see the look of fear on her face. She said something in Chinese. Yanmei answered softly, putting a comforting hand on the shorter woman's shoulder. They hugged, and the servant found a seat in the corner, away from the withered body of the dead Forsaken, the one that Terry had killed without using his hands.

Kirkus made sure that no one had taken the Forsaken's body away. He considered it a reminder of what Terry Henry Walton was capable of. Yanmei ignored it, but her servant was uncomfortable and averted her eyes.

"She will come too, of course, to a place where she'll live free. We don't have servants in North Chicago," Terry said smoothly, trying to keep his voice free from judgment.

"What if that's what she wants to do?" Yanmei asked pointedly.

"Then she'll be free to do it. Let me revise my earlier statement. Everyone is free to find their own destiny. The only thing we require is that everyone works, everyone gives back to the community in some way," Terry explained.

"You are a communist, like those in old China?" Yanmei asked.

"NO!" Terry blurted. He'd thought about that over the past thirty years, but hadn't expected to deliver an answer.

"I'm sorry. Communism is a political system. I would say that we probably have something more like socialism, or a free society that is heavily taxed. We used to contribute everything to a central pool, but now, it's less than half. We have the dining hall and that is the main focus of it all. As long as people can eat regularly, then everything else becomes possible."

In his mind, Terry had looked through a mountain of history books regarding political and economic systems.

None of it was exciting reading, but he found it all fascinating. He'd recognized a trend early in his studies.

"Most systems have their merits, just until the leadership is corrupted. No, we don't have elections, but the mayor consistently does what is in the best interest of the people. I guess I'm the self-appointed overseer. Have been ever since my first meeting with Billy Spires. I've done things that I will spend the rest of my life making up for. Kirkus called it a moral compass. I call it a conscience that will never be satisfied with my apologies."

Terry was opening up to Yanmei in his continuing efforts to gain her confidence. Kirkus only had the pain of failure to offer. Terry was talking about the power of freedom.

And Terry was starting to like this captor, not because of Stockholm syndrome, but because of her simple act of calming her servant. She was providing a promised level of protection. She made her servant feel safe without being afraid to ask for that security. He also felt that she was as much Kirkus's prisoner as he was.

"Kirkus will fall, because his style of control cannot survive the new world. We won't let it. I won't allow it. Maybe that's why I'm here. He lost eight of his minions to capture and one, almost two more attempting to restrain me." Terry nodded toward the body on the floor. "He must have calculated that it was worth the cost. What does that tell you?"

Yanmei shook her head.

Another explosion shook the walls. This one was closer.

❖ ❖ ❖

Joseph laughed as dust filled the air. Gene roared his disapproval once again at the noise of the explosion.

"I read your goddamned book!" Joseph yelled. He'd seen the trap and tossed a large rock to activate it.

"Next time, fucknuts, give us a warning!" Char yelled, her ears still ringing from the power of the blast. They were almost at the end of Houchins Narrows, which led into the area known as the Rotunda, a massive open space rounded from eons past when water circled within.

Char stayed behind Joseph as he walked from the tunnel into the Rotunda.

Behind her, a man screamed while another started

shooting. Mark yelled to cease fire.

"What the fuck are you shooting at?" Mark yelled.

"Something took Glen," another replied. Char looked back. One of the privates was aiming his rifle at the tunnel wall. She hadn't seen any side passages.

The lighting was still on despite the explosions. Char expected they would lose that benefit of illumination when it was most inconvenient.

"Flashlights!" she called. Some of the Force warriors started winding furiously. Others had taken the ride on the pod to charge their flashlights. A number of beams appeared, clearly outlined in the dust floating through the cave. They danced along the wall until they all converged on a single spot.

"There's a tunnel here," Mark said loudly, motioning for the warrior aiming the rifle to join him. "Blood on the rock. Hang on. Cover me. Wait, you got silver bullets in that thing?"

The man changed magazines, ejected the current round, and sent a new one home. Mark was not amused. "Get your head out of your ass, or you're going to end up just like him," Mark growled, pointing at the wall.

The captain worked his way inside, then dragged a body out. Glen's head had been bashed in. Mark cursed silently, then carefully propped Glen's body against the wall, making it look like he was resting. He waved the warriors away from the narrow tunnel mouth.

"Fire in the hole!" he said as he tossed a grenade inside, dove away, and slapped his hands over his ears. The explosion sent debris from the tunnel and created yet another dust cloud. Mark looked at the cave wall, waving his hand to clear the air.

He gave Char the thumbs up. "Move it out," he called.

They'd pick up Glen's body during the retrograde once the mission was complete. If they didn't survive, then at least Glen was comfortable in his final resting place.

No one contemplated anything differently. They always planned to win.

Char tomahawked her hand in the direction of an outlet on the other side of the Rotunda. Joseph looked at the walls as he and Gene moved further into the open area.

The sound of metal caressing metal alerted them. Gene and Joseph stood back to back as a thousand metal discs, sharp as razors, flew into the cavern.

◈ ◈ ◈

NORTH CHICAGO

Felicity and Marcie dragged Billy through the door. His eyes were wide with shock and his breathing ragged.

The sound of gunfire filled the area in front of the mayor's building. Kim and Kae were out there. Marcie was beside herself. Marcie and Kae's kids were already in the mayor's office hiding under the desk.

"Come!" she yelled in their direction. They were too afraid to move.

Billy started shaking as spasms wracked his body. His jaws clenched and pink foam bubbled from his mouth. He stiffened, jerked twice, and relaxed as a long sigh signaled his final breath.

Felicity screamed in anguish. Marcie started to cry but forced herself to stand and run into the mayor's office to grab her two children. She carried the youngest on her hip while holding the other's hand.

The children were terrified and panicking. Marcie wrestled with Mary Ellen and finally had to pick her up, too. Liam had his head buried against Marcie's breast, his small body jerking as he sobbed uncontrollably.

"Come on!" Marcie yelled at her mother through tear-filled eyes.

Felicity looked up, nodded, and stood, still hanging onto Billy's hand.

"Leave him!" Marcie bumped her mother and headed for the stairs.

With one last look, Felicity turned and ran after her daughter.

❖ ❖ ❖

The enemy's Forsaken were projecting terror in every direction, sweeping the minds of the North Chicago residents. Most of the warriors from the Force were affected, although some were able to fight it off. Joseph had helped them to understand the mind control that some Forsaken were capable of.

Those few warriors were fighting back while the rest of the Force were running. Kirkus's human minions weren't ready to fight professional soldiers, so it took no time at all to eliminate that threat. The survivors were either still running or cowering in a hole somewhere; their fear was real, not created by a Forsaken.

Kim and Kae had received more training than anyone else, even members of the Force. It was the benefit of being Terry and Char's children.

The two stood side by side, ready to fight, as two Forsaken approached. The other two Vampires were left to deal with the four Werewolves that emerged from one of Akio's pods.

Timmons, Sue, Shonna, and Ted scowled as they approached. The two Forsaken laughed.

"Were-fucking-wolves," one said arrogantly.

Timmons and Sue walked an arm's length apart. They liked the Forsaken to be overconfident. On cue, they ran at the Forsaken closest to them.

He flexed his knees and raised his fists as if preparing to wade into a boxing ring.

Timmons attacked first with all the power he could muster. The Forsaken realized at that instant that he'd made a horrible mistake. The Werewolf's blow drove the Forsaken's own fist backward into his face hard enough to jar his front teeth loose.

Sue spun as she arrived and kicked the Forsaken so hard in the groin that it shattered his pelvis. He went down in a heap. Timmons stopped on a dime, turned, and with his knife, slashed the creature's throat, cut the skin and muscle around his neck, and twisted the head until it came free from the spine.

Five seconds start to finish, alive and uninjured to headless.

Three Forsaken remained.

Ted and Shonna were engaged with the Forsaken that had intercepted them, but their fight wasn't going as well.

Ted was furiously trading blows, but the Forsaken was easily blocking them while dodging to keep Ted between him and Shonna.

"Get out of my way!" Shonna barked. Ted was the least capable of all the Werewolves when it came to hand-to-hand combat. He hardly ever trained and whined the whole time whenever they made him attend.

The others had improved to the point that they were more deadly in human form. Ted knew what he had to do. He jumped back and cleared the way for Shonna to engage. The Forsaken considered her a lesser opponent and stood up straight as if to fight her that way.

She jabbed once before pounding his chin with a vicious

uppercut. His head snapped backward. She followed with a kick to the groin and kneed his face as he went down.

A Werewolf growled as it dove in and grabbed the Forsaken by the throat, rending and shaking. Shonna left Ted to it.

She joined Timmons and Sue as they ran for the final two Forsaken.

Kim and Kae had just engaged, but the Forsaken were physically faster and stronger. Only the young humans' training gave them any hope. They weren't able to find an opening, only block, and block, and block some more.

They danced back and forth, their counterpunches easily repulsed.

It dawned on Kaeden that none of the Forsaken were armed, although the humans from the pod were. He didn't understand it and recognized it as meaningless in his current situation. He knew that the Forsaken wanted to capture him and Kimber alive.

They wouldn't have used weapons on the young adults regardless.

That meant the Kim and Kae could take greater risks while fighting. Their lives were not on the line.

Kimber fought like one possessed. She rained blow after blow toward the Forsaken, but he brushed them away as if annoyed by a fly. His attacks took all of her attention, and although she tried to counterpunch, the Forsaken was unimpressed. He wore her down and pressed in.

Kae could do nothing to help her as he was fighting his own losing battle.

He thought he could hear the wolf pack howling as they approached. There was rifle fire. There was screaming. Time slowed to a crawl. He heard the sound of a fist impacting flesh, but he couldn't look to see who landed the punch, his sister or her enemy.

Then all the sounds died away until the only thing he could hear was his own labored breathing and his pulse pounding in his ears. His vision narrowed until he could only see the Forsaken standing before him.

Kae grunted as something rammed into his stomach, but his sight remained locked on the blackness of the Forsaken's eyes. He saw the fist coming at him, and then all of a sudden, the Forsaken was gone. Kae dropped to his knees, closed his eyes, retched, and fell over.

CHAPTER SIXTEEN

MAMMOTH CAVE

Gene rolled around on the floor of the cavern, caking his wounds with a bloody mud pack.

Joseph staggered a few steps and stopped, looking like he was going to pass out. Char rushed in, wary of the ledges around the Rotunda. Small discs lay everywhere, crunching metal on stone as she stepped on them.

"I'm not sure that could have sucked more," Joseph mumbled, using one of Terry's favorite expressions. His leather clothes were shredded, and he was bleeding profusely.

"Here," Char said and took out her flask. He drank, but they both knew what he really needed if he was to heal quickly.

"This will have to do, fucker. Deal with it." Char ripped the flask from his hands. "I thought you could detect the traps?"

She was angry and glaring at him.

"He only had to get lucky once. I had to get lucky every time," Joseph tried to explain, unable to meet Char's intense, glowing-purple glare. "Can you feel it?"

Char stopped glaring and cocked her head. She'd been too distracted.

"TH," she whispered.

"Caution, beautiful Werewolf!" Joseph said with a spurt of renewed vigor. "The closer we get, the slower we must go, the more we must spread out, and the more vulnerable we will be."

"Prophetic words, Joseph. Are you able to lead us down?" she asked.

"No," he replied as his eyes rolled back in his head and he started to fall.

"DAMMIT!" Char bellowed, and the echoes were deafening. She caught Joseph and helped him to the ground. She laid him down with his head propped against a natural stone bench.

Gene grumbled. His Werebear form had weathered the razor storm much better than Joseph's leathers. He ambled forward. Char caught up with him and walked at his side as they headed out of the Rotunda and down Broadway.

A voice from behind called to them.

"Sorry it took so long to catch up, but *you* can't be on point, my alpha," Adams told her. He moved in front, working his way around the injured Werebear. Once Adams was in the lead, some distance from the others, he cautiously moved forward, stopping every few steps to sniff first and then highlight spots on the wall with his flashlight.

"The closer we get, the slower we must go," Adams said softly to himself. "Who would have thought that a Forsaken would guide us, wisely, in an effort to save our lives?"

Char thought about the words. There was a secondary tunnel off the Rotunda. "Captain! Seal that tunnel," Char ordered.

"Aye, aye, ma'am," Mark said, the sound loud within the echo chamber of the Rotunda.

He looked at one of the privates and smiled. "Satchel charge," he said, nodding and biting his lip. The private pulled it from his pack and handed it over.

"Cover me, you and you." He pointed to two members of the squad. They aimed their rifles down the unlit passageway. One fired two shots.

"Cease fire!" Mark yelled. "What are you shooting at?"

"I saw someone in there!" the private yelled back, never taking his eye from the rear sight of his M4 Carbine.

Mark shook his head. "It doesn't matter. Fire in the hole!"

Mark pulled the cord and sent the charge winging down the passageway. It hit the side wall as it entered, not going anywhere near as far as he wanted. The three warriors ran for it, diving after counting to five and covering their heads. The concussive blast from the charge was mostly expended outward into the Rotunda, but enough of it blasted the walls of the secondary tunnel to shake loose a great pillar of rock that fell into the entrance, blocking the tunnel. Mark stood up and dusted himself off.

"Well?" he demanded of the other two still face down on the cave floor. "What are you waiting for?"

The two privates popped up and returned to the line of warriors heading toward Broadway.

"Two by two, ladies!" Mark called out, ordering the warriors to operate in pairs.

Merrit hung back to help out if any Forsaken showed up near the rear of the formation.

"Forward," Char said softly, pointing toward Broadway, the tunnel that continued into the bowels of the earth.

In the silence of the cave, everyone heard the order.

❖ ❖ ❖

TERRY'S PRISON

"What's your friend's name?" Terry asked. Yanmei looked into the corner where her servant sat hugging her knees to her chest.

"Her name is Fu," Yanmei finally answered.

"The sooner we leave, the better off we'll be," Terry suggested, trying to not sound desperate. He wasn't sure he was successful.

The Weretiger smacked her lips and folded her arms across her chest. She leaned against the wall, her head tipped backward. Terry read her body language as being defensive.

He'd been too aggressive.

"Where'd you grow up, Yanmei?" Terry asked. She relaxed, but didn't uncross her arms.

She was still on the defensive, protecting herself.

When she answered, it wasn't what Terry expected.

"Does it matter?" she started, keeping her arms crossed but looking down as she shifted her feet. "Does anything matter after the fall? Here I am, doing this! I should be in a city on the edge of a jungle, living two lives, both fruitful, rather than wasting away inside this cave! But we lost our freedom of choice when the world ended, didn't we?"

She looked to be talking to the floor. Terry was no longer in the conversation. He worked his shoulders, hoping that when the time came, he would be able to wrap his arms around his wife and children. He kept his mouth closed.

"Of course we did. Those with the power over life and death were the only ones capable of making decisions. The rest of us just went along. What else was there to do?" she cried.

She uncrossed her arms, held her face in her hands briefly, and then ran her fingers through her straight black hair. When she looked up, she locked Terry Henry in her gaze.

"Those with the so-called power need people like you to do their bidding. Then you run across people like me. The only thing that I demand is that people be themselves," Terry said softly, leaning forward against his chains. He believed in what he was saying because he lived it. "Maybe I insist that they be the best version of themselves."

He thought of Betty and Lester and their three cows, what a pain in the ass they'd been.

Terry opened his eyes. As thoughts did, his memories of Betty and Lester had flashed through his mind over the course of an instant. Yanmei hadn't moved since he last looked.

When she did move, she dropped her hands to her side, smiled at Terry Henry, and nodded.

❖ ❖ ❖

MAMMOTH CAVE

Kirkus intended to ambush the drawn out line of intruders. He'd gotten one but was driven deeper into the tunnels when the grenade exploded. Before that, he thought he heard the human in charge yelling something about silver-tipped ammunition.

That could be a problem.

He was in the tunnel off the Rotunda when they decided to blow it. Kirkus was ready to take out those three idiots before anyone realized that he'd been there, but they were aiming their rifles, and then one fired, narrowly missing his head. Kirkus was not yet ready to experience the pain of having silver punched through his body.

He would count on the next series of trips and traps to whittle the numbers down.

Kirkus had also been dismayed by the presence of a Forsaken with the party. He couldn't imagine what would drive a Forsaken to join Terry Henry and his group. He couldn't imagine Terry Henry allowing the Forsaken to feed on human blood as his kind was destined to do.

Forsaken were higher on the food chain, as Kirkus saw it.

He ran when they threw the satchel charge, but it got caught at the entrance to the tunnel. After the explosion and the group had moved down Broadway, Kirkus found that he could get through the rubble and into the Rotunda.

He worked his way out of the tunnel and waited until the last of the Force members disappeared into the next cave before approaching the Forsaken lying on the floor.

Kirkus strode boldly up to him.

"A daywalker," he sneered, standing with his hands on his hips, looming over the injured Forsaken.

"My name is Joseph," he said as he forced his eyes open and looked up. He slowly moved his hand to his head so he could remove his hat. Joseph was surprised that he wasn't afraid. The Forsaken before him was more powerful, radiating an aura that others would sit up and take notice of.

"Why?"

"Name?" Joseph responded as tersely.

"Kirkus," he said as if it sullied his name to give it to one such as Joseph.

"Well, Kirkus, it's like this. Terry Henry Walton saved my life. The Werewolf pack was going to tear me apart, and he wouldn't let them. Over the years, he trained me how to fight, but alas, I find myself at a disadvantage after that razor storm you set up. My compliments to your ingenuity on that, by the way," Joseph said with a slight nod.

A smile twitched at the corner of Kirkus's mouth, but he quickly tamped it down.

"When they are all dead, I will give you the option of joining me. Until then, Joseph," Kirkus said, walking away until he disappeared over the rubble and into the side tunnel as he raced to get in front of the intruders.

Joseph watched him go. His whole body hurt, but he needed to get back into the fight. Clovis brayed in the distance, echoing up and down the tunnels. He smiled.

"Humans and their dogs."

◈ ◈ ◈

NORTH CHICAGO

Kae opened his eyes. He was on his knees at the bottom of the steps to the mayor's building. Shonna and the Forsaken were rolling on the ground in a life and death struggle.

Timmons and Sue were both wailing mercilessly on another Forsaken not far from where Kae was coming back to himself. Kimber was dancing around the outside, chancing a kick when an opening presented itself.

The Forsaken was no longer able to protect itself. Kae was amazed that it was still standing.

"Shonna!" he managed to yell. Kim heard her brother and turned, seeing that he was alert, even though he remained on his knees. She slapped Sue on the back and they both ran to the other fight, grabbing the Forsaken and dragging it off Shonna.

She was bleeding from a number of cuts and bites, but they only made her angry. Shonna rolled to all fours and jumped to her feet.

Kim and Sue had the Forsaken's arms behind him and were pressing his face into the ground. Shonna vaulted into the air and dropped a pile driver kick into his head. The Forsaken's skull shattered, and its brains splattered in all directions.

Sue jumped back, but it was too late.

"What the hell?" she exclaimed, wiping her hands on the Forsaken's dirty clothes. The disgust on Kimber's face told them how she felt about Shonna's final solution.

"Sorry," Shonna mumbled, not looking sorry at all.

Ted howled from near the second pod, and his wolf pack replied. They were tracking the intruders.

The warriors had returned to their senses. They were running to reclaim dropped weapons and establish a blocking force in front of the mayor's building.

Kae stood when his head cleared. He didn't have to wonder what had happened. The Forsaken, when it was face-to-face with him, had taken over his mind. Kae remembered the internal struggle. The Vampire had not been completely successful.

Kimber grabbed her brother by the shoulders, finishing wiping her hands clean on his shirt. He'd find out later about that, but at present, they were both safe and healthy.

"The kids," he realized.

"Inside!" she exclaimed, bolting away. He struggled to get one foot in front of the other, stumbling as he climbed the steps.

As soon as they entered, they heard the yelling from upstairs, the rough voices. The intruders had gotten inside the mayor's building.

And Billy lay dead in the hallway.

Kaeden caught up to Kim, where they stopped for a moment before both running for the stairway.

CHAPTER SEVENTEEN

MAMMOTH CAVE

It took the group a long time to transit Broadway, but the area was so large, a booby trap would have been minimally effective. From Broadway, a number of side tunnels branched off. One still had a sign for the restroom.

"FUCK!" Char howled, growing more frustrated by the options and the snail's pace at which they moved.

She sniffed the air, then closed her eyes and reached into the etheric. She could feel that Terry was somewhere in front of them, in or near the main tunnel. She could sense both Forsaken and humans in the side tunnels, but not many of the living beings.

She could also sense a Weretiger near Terry. She assumed the Were was acting as a guard. "You'll get your chance to fight a Weretiger, Gene," Char snarled, complete with lip curl.

Aaron shifted uncomfortably, padding back and forth in his Weretiger form. He'd already sensed one of his kind. He had been accepted into the pack, thanks to the kindness of Chief Foxtail, but he had always been alone. The FDG had traveled to China often since Aaron had joined the community, but he deplored how Akio, Terry, and Char instantly assumed Weretigers were the enemy.

He conceded that Weretigers were an aggressive bunch and after Gene was almost killed, they took no chances. It was time for Aaron to put it on the line.

Aaron threw his head around, nodding down the tunnel, padding ahead, then coming back. He stood and put his paws on Cory's shoulders. She grunted under his weight, even though he was a lean cat. Cory could feel his sadness. She put a hand on his arm.

"I think we should let Aaron talk with the other Weretiger first, Mother," Cory said supportively.

"When we get close, I'll consider it," Char replied as she looked back and forth. "Mark. Grenades."

She didn't need to say anything else. The warriors closest to the side tunnels cleared the area in front, yelled, "Fire in the hole," and blasted the tunnels.

Most of the tunnels weren't blocked, but with the explosions, Char hoped that anyone trying to get in behind them would be dissuaded. She didn't want to fight within the side tunnels or the main tunnel. She simply wanted to get TH and leave.

They'd already suffered enough.

They'd passed through Broadway and tensions were still high. Merrit fell back, even with the last warrior, as he used his senses to help him see an ambusher should one try to sneak up on them.

Adams crept into Gothic Avenue, a long tunnel with a number of washouts and offshoot tunnels that fell away into the darkness far below. He shined his flashlight, looking for hiding demons, even though his senses told him there was no one there.

He moved forward in hops, leaping from one place to another as he remained wary.

The first rumble passed in only an instant. Everyone froze. Adams felt it in his feet. He was closest to the sound and the vibration. When he realized what it was, it was too late.

Adams relaxed as the cave floor, a natural bridge, separated and started to fall.

Gene was on the split, throwing himself flat as the world before him fell. His bigger haunches kept him from going face first over the edge.

"NO!" Char yelled, running toward the trap.

Adams didn't scream as he disappeared into the darkness. He said only one word. "Xandrie."

Char took a knee and hung her head. Above her on the wall of the cave was a sign that read, "Bottomless Pit." She closed her eyes and reached out with her senses, following the living Werewolf downward, longer than should have been possible. When he finally hit bottom, his life force was extinguished.

Cory held her mother, pulled her upright. "We need to keep going. Father is up there somewhere." Cordelia's eyes glowed blue in the dim light.

When Char looked up, her own glowed a vivid purple. Rage seethed within, and Char was about to turn it loose.

❖ ❖ ❖

Yanmei was torn. So many small explosions and they were getting closer. She closed her eyes and could feel them coming.

"A Weretiger?" she asked.

Terry shook his head. If Aaron was with them, that meant Cordelia was there, too. He wasn't good with that. He needed out of his restraints so he could get his daughter away from Kirkus's house of horrors.

"Yes. His name is Aaron. He was a teacher in China when he was modified. He came back to the United States before the fall, but he was always an outcast. We brought him into the pack and consider him one of our family, but he's still alone. He loves teaching, so he's taught all of our children in addition to most of the kids in North Chicago!" Terry tried to end on a high note.

"I miss my own kind, too," Yanmei whispered. "The Sacred Clan. I miss them. They were scattered to the winds in the final days."

"Let's go meet him. Unchain me, please, Yanmei. We need to get out of here!" Terry knew that he couldn't share that his daughter was with her mother but expected that Kirkus already knew. He wondered where the Forsaken was. As they got close, Terry figured that Kirkus would show up.

Terry didn't want to be in chains when that happened.

The Weretiger nodded slightly, looked at her servant, and then walked up to Terry, grabbing a shackle in both hands.

❖ ❖ ❖

Kim and Kae took the steps three at a time as they headed to the second floor. There were more floors above, but they weren't being used. The mayor had her home on the second floor, and that was where the yelling was coming from.

Kim and Kae ran down the hallway, but Kae held out an arm to stop his sister before bursting into the middle of a bad situation. They put their ears to the closed door and listened, even though their own hard breathing and pounding hearts worked against them.

The men were yelling at Felicity and Marcie, ordering them to put something down. The kids were terrified and screaming.

From what Kae could tell, the men had their backs to the door. Kae motioned to his sister, then did a finger countdown from three to one. After flashing the last digit, he turned the knob, and they both slammed into the locked door.

"Crap!" Kae yelled, then pushed his sister to the side as he dove the other way.

Gunfire echoed from the room as bullets ripped through the door and chipped the wall on the other side of the hallway. Kaeden and Kimber stood with their backs to the thick wall on either side of the door. Kim glared at her brother.

Neither of them had a weapon, but even if they had, they would never fire into the room where Kae's family was.

"You're surrounded!" Kim called toward the door.

"Maybe," a man's voice said from the other side of the door. "But we have some people in here who say that you're going to let us go."

"I'm pretty sure they didn't say that," Kim replied. "Your buddies are all dead. It's just you two dickweeds."

Kae looked angrily at his sister, then held his hands out, mouthing the words, "What the fuck?"

She waved him away.

"You have two choices. Let them go so we can talk about your future in North Chicago, or we'll just have to kill you," Kim said coldly.

"I don't think you're going to do that. If we're going to die, then we'll just make sure these pretty ladies die, too. Hey, Bob, do you think those kids will bounce if we toss them out the window?" the one voice called from behind the door.

"Maybe we'll try one at a time, to check things out," a second voice answered. Neither was laughing. Kae hoped that everyone was bluffing and that things would calm down.

But just in case…

Kae ran past the door. Another shot and more splintering as the bullet ripped through, but Kaeden was already long past.

He ran down the hallway, down the steps, and out the front door. Kae almost ran Timmons down.

"They have my kids," he panted, unable to explain further.

Timmons grabbed the young man's shoulder. "Then we have some work left to do," he said calmly, his face set. Sue's lip curled of its own volition.

Wolves howled nearby, followed by a rifle shot and a man's scream. Ted looked into the distance.

Shonna was standing nearby, looming over a dead and rapidly shriveling Forsaken. She left it and joined Kaeden and the two Werewolves.

"The door is locked upstairs. They threatened to throw my kids out the window!" Kae said in a panic.

"I'll be there to catch them if they do," Shonna vowed

and jogged away to take a position below the window, but there were many to choose from. She stopped and held up her hands. "Which one?"

Kae pointed. Shonna dashed to it.

"I think I've had enough of these assholes," Sue stated.

"I'm with you, my love. Let's go unfuck this." Timmons fiercely kissed Sue, and they ran for the door. Once inside, they stripped and changed into Werewolves. Kae ran past them, but they beat him up the steps.

They waited near the door. In Werewolf form, they doubted they could break it down, but Kim and Kae had been well-trained in how to breach a locked door. Kae jogged down the hallway, stopping short of the entry.

He dropped to all fours and crawled, well below the bullet holes. He crouched, popped up, and back-kicked the door at the point of the lock, bursting it inward. He dove to the side as two Werewolves flew past him.

A single shot rang out, thudding into a meaty target, but with a growl and jaws snapping, the next sound was of a rifle clattering to the floor.

Kim and Kae leaned into the doorway and looked inside. Felicity and Marcie were hugging the children and pulling them aside as two frenzied Werewolves killed their prey.

With a few final shakes, they each dropped a dead body to the floor. Timmons and Sue changed back into human form, standing naked and covered in blood.

Kim went into a side room where she knew towels were stored, bringing one each for Timmons and Sue. The Werewolves had never cared about being naked in front of other people.

They still didn't care as they wiped themselves off. Timmons threw the towel over his shoulder, but Sue wrapped up.

Felicity, Marcie, and Kae were too distracted by hugging each other to notice.

"Come on, Uncle Timmons," Kimber said, adding a stink-eye for emphasis. "And thank you both," she added softly, while trying to usher Felicity, Marcie, Kae, and the kids out of the room.

They made their way downstairs and outside. Kim grabbed Sergeant Boris. "There are two bodies in the mayor's private rooms upstairs. Get them out of there and clean up the blood. And the former mayor is in the hallway downstairs. With reverence, send a detail to cover him with a sheet and bring him out. We have work to do burning the wicked while celebrating the life of Billy Spires, Mayor of both New Boulder and North Chicago," Kimber told him.

◈ ◈ ◈

Ted was alone. He'd changed back into human form and gotten dressed. He was sitting on the ramp of the intruders' pod. The FDG had set up a perimeter in case there was another incursion, but Ted was certain there would not be any more.

They only had one vehicle when they snatched Terry Henry earlier that morning.

Ted looked into the pod, nearly identical to the ones they used, but there was a difference. This one smelled like death.

The Werewolf tucked his nose inside his shirt as he boarded to check the systems. He tapped on the interface and it came to life. He had watched Akio operate the system for more than twenty-five years, but had never gotten the opportunity to operate it himself.

He'd always been too reserved to ask. But now, he was free to dig into it.

Ted pulled up screen after screen, finding the interface simplistic for one of his intellect. He started digging deeper, wanting to see into the ones and zeros of Kurtherian technology.

The system wouldn't let him get there, but he kept trying.

He wondered if access would change in flight. So he closed the rear ramp and took the pod skyward.

Ted programmed the flight computer to take him back to Mammoth Cave. He worked the interface, not noticing the acceleration as the craft raced into the southeastern sky.

CHAPTER EIGHTEEN

TERRY'S PRISON

can't get the lock undone. Oh, no! He's going to know, and you can't help me!" Yanmei accused TH. "Why did I start to trust you?"

She kept fumbling with the lock. Terry knew that he could pick it, if only he had a hand free.

"Relax. You need two thin strips of stiff metal. Or a bolt cutters," he suggested. She glared at him. "I'm sorry, but you're committed now, and the best chance you have to save yourself is by freeing me. Now go find something before he comes back!"

She was terrified and it showed, having lost the confidence of her earlier persona. Fu was cowering in the corner, covering her head with her hands.

"Does she understand English?" Terry asked.

Yanmei shook her head.

"Then she doesn't know you tried to release me. Yell at

me in Chinese that my chains are tight and that I'll never escape. Then call me names and spit on me or kick me. In her mind, all she'll think about is how you have done your duty."

Yanmei thought for a moment, then nodded almost imperceptibly. She started screaming at Terry, then spun and tagged him mid-chest with a wild roundhouse kick.

He gasped in pain at the unexpected impact. He thought she would pull the kick, but she didn't. She hit him with everything she had. Terry saw Fu look up.

Yanmei ordered her to do something as the smaller woman bowed and although scared, she opened the door and bolted. The door stood open as the Weretiger continued to berate a stunned Terry Henry Walton.

She stopped when she felt that her servant was sufficiently far away, in a direction opposite of where Kirkus was in a secondary tunnel that led from Broadway to the Giant's Coffin in the chamber next to the hospital ruins where Terry's prison room had been carved.

"Where's my stuff?" Terry wondered aloud.

"He has it. You don't need it so don't think about it," she cautioned.

My whip and knife, Terry thought. *Relics from the past. They can be replaced. We need to get out of here.*

❖ ❖ ❖

MAMMOTH CAVE

Char gracefully moved to the front of the formation. She walked as if her feet weren't even touching the stone floor. She trod lightly to avoid triggering any more traps, but she moved with a deadly purpose.

The bridge had fallen, but a narrower strip of stone remained. A wire along the wall signaled how the Forsaken and his minions had moved through this tunnel without causing a collapse. A permanent trap for the unwary.

Or maybe it had always been weak, and the collapsing bridge wasn't a trap at all.

Cory was almost as light on her feet as she moved to the front, followed closely by Aaron, but Gene growled and blocked their way with his body. He stood on two feet, almost filling this section of the cavern. The Werebear hobbled along behind Char, keeping one paw wrapped tightly around the wire.

Cordelia tried to close in behind Gene, but a warrior held her back. "If he falls, he's going to tear that wire out of the wall," he whispered.

She nodded, itching to catch up. When Gene stepped onto the solid floor of the other side, Cory was off like a shot, almost running along the narrow ledge. Aaron danced after her, studiously avoiding looking down, while Clovis ran along the edge, completely immune to the fear of falling.

Char moved on. Terry's aura was growing in her mind, and the Forsaken was not between her and her husband. He was below them and running parallel.

The Weretiger was still with TH. She was close, but he was alive. With each step that Char took, she closed the distance between them.

Gene joined her as she continued down the long and relatively straight Gothic Avenue.

Char stopped and grabbed a handful of Werebear fur to keep him from walking past. He groaned as he sniffed and looked without seeing anything. Char picked up a small boulder and rolled it down the middle of the tunnel. It rolled until it angled away from the crowned floor and bounced off the wall a couple times, coming to a stop fifty feet from where Char stood.

She repeated her trap-finding efforts, settling for throwing a handful of rocks at the wall. The fireworks started on the second throw when a gout of flame burst from the wall, filling the tunnel in front of them with fire.

Char grabbed Cory and dove to the ground. As fire continued to belch into the tunnel, it became difficult to breathe. The acrid smoke trailed along the ceiling until it found its way out.

"Hit the deck!" Mark's order echoed down the tunnel.

It became difficult to see as the smoke burned their eyes.

"Keep your eyes closed," Char told her daughter. Cory didn't argue as she struggled to breathe, even with holding her shirt over her mouth and nose.

Someone started firing at the back of the formation. Char couldn't see who or where.

"Target!" a voice called, followed by more gunfire.

"Target!" a second voice called before he opened up into a void in the tunnel wall.

Char concentrated, not finding any lifeforms. There shouldn't have been any targets, but she had to trust that the warriors had seen something.

"Cease fire!" the captain called. "What the fuck are you idiots firing at?" Mark crouched as he stalked up and down the line of warriors.

"That's just smoke, you morons! Stop wasting ammo!" Mark bellowed before giving the "all clear."

❖ ❖ ❖

MARTELLE AND ANDERLE

THE LANDING PAD OUTSIDE MAMMOTH CAVE

First Sergeant Blevin sat next to Corporal Heitz. They watched the only ground avenue of approach to the pods that led in the direction of the cave entrance. They'd turned the jeep off to save fuel while they waited.

"Keep your finger off the trigger. The first people up that path are going to be ours. You mark my words," Blevin told his old friend.

"My baby doesn't have a trigger, only this beautiful butterfly lever. And I haven't cocked it yet, either, so cool your jets," Max replied with a cackle.

"I'm glad we got to come along, and I'm glad I didn't have to walk anywhere. That would be a huge pain in my ass," Blevin said.

"Doing any work is a pain in your ass, has been for the past forty years, you lazy bastard," Max quipped as he leaned heavily against the jeep's roll bar. He breathed deeply of the fresh Kentucky air. "I like it here, Blevin. The air is nice and clean."

"Bah. This is the first time we've left North Chicago in decades. You like it because it's different, but then you won't like it because it's different. What about dinner? What will you do without Claire's Diner?"

"Hmm. Starve, I suppose," Max conceded. "Fair enough. It's nice, but I like what I like, and that's Mayra's cooking."

"Don't we all, my friend," Blevin agreed.

"Incoming!" Gerry called.

Max grabbed the lever and attempted to cock the ma deuce, but he couldn't pull it hard enough. "Dammit! Come on, you bitch!" Max struggled until Blevin jumped up to help.

Together they yanked the cocking handle back and down. Max wrapped his fingers around the spade handles and let his thumb hover over the butterfly trigger. His head swiveled left and right, up and down.

"I'm not seeing anything, Blevin. Where are they?" Max asked calmly.

A shadow descended over the jeep. "Fuckers got in behind us, Max! Light 'em up!"

Corporal Heitz swiveled the gun mount and leaned down to lift the barrel of the fifty cal to aim at the target overhead. He depressed the lever and the machine gun barked, sending a stream of bullets into the hovering pod.

The aircraft banked away violently. Max let off the lever and thrust his hand in the air, a single digit propped skyward. "Fuck off, you bastards!"

"You showed 'em, Max. Fuck off, goobers!" Blevin chimed in from the driver's seat.

❖ ❖ ❖

The pod arrived, and Ted hovered over the area until he saw the other pods in a small clearing. He expertly flew the short distance and slowed as he looked for a place to land.

The fifty caliber bullets clanging on the hull surprised him, making him drag a finger across the control screen. The pod jumped and slid sideways. Had it not been for the fail-safes, the pod would have crashed into those on the ground.

Ted steadied the pod. The bullets weren't going to penetrate the hull of the pod, which was built to withstand the heat of the atmosphere, as well as strikes from micro-meteors.

Ted crept back toward the other pods. He activated the

external speakers. "Why are you shooting at me?" he asked.

"Oh crap!" Max exclaimed. "Why didn't you tell me that was one of ours?"

"You old bastard! You're the one hammering the *butter-fly trigger*. I oughta punch you right in your old crusty face," Blevin threatened.

"I'll save you the trouble." Max slid under the roll bar, showing surprising dexterity. He took a ham-handed swing at Blevin, who dodged it by leaning backward and falling out of the jeep.

Max followed him out until the two oldsters were rolling around in the dirt.

"You ever see anything like that?" Sergeant Nickles asked the warrior next to him. The young woman shook her head as she cradled her rifle before her.

The sergeant cupped his hands around his mouth and projected his voice as strongly as he could. "Land it right here, Ted! LAND HERE!" Nickles chopped his arm down and pointed to the small open area.

Ted tickled the controls, turning the pod and dropping it quickly to land lightly into the tight space. He lowered the ramp and strolled into the open air.

"Where's everybody else?" Sergeant Nickles asked.

"Oh," Ted replied, turning back to look into the empty pod.

❖ ❖ ❖

Terry sighed in relief when Fu returned. Yanmei greeted the young woman in Chinese and took the tools that she had brought. As an afterthought, Yanmei closed the door and had Fu lean against it.

With the proper equipment and Terry talking her through it, the first shackle unclasped. Terry gasped when he lowered his arm, the first time in untold hours.

She unlocked the other shackle in seconds.

"Thank you," Terry said sincerely, rolling his shoulders and flexing his muscles. "Where is he?"

The Weretiger closed her eyes and clenched her jaw tightly. "Oh no," she whispered.

The door burst inward, sending Fu flying across the room and sprawling over the withered corpse. She screamed as she scrambled to free herself. Yanmei opened her mouth and hissed. Kirkus's eyes blazed with his fury.

Terry's glowed a faint red. He had been given his chance to fight for his life. "Come on, asswipe, we've got business," Terry snarled.

❖ ❖ ❖

MAMMOTH CAVE

Char sensed that the Forsaken had joined Terry and the Weretiger. "We need to hurry," she said over her shoulder. Gene grumbled from behind her.

Cory wasn't pleased. "Joseph said the closer we get, the slower we have to go. We can't get in a hurry now!" she said louder than she intended.

Char hesitated. She made a fist and watched it shake. The fury and frustration were seething just below the surface. She had no patience left.

"Merrit, get up here!" she growled.

"Yes, my alpha," came the immediate response. Even at the rear of the line of warriors, he could sense her rage. It was only that morning that she shattered Timmons's face for a slight affront.

Only that morning.

Since then, Adams had been killed, Akio and Joseph were both down, and Gene was injured. As he worked his way to the front, he wondered how much more blood it would cost to free Terry Henry Walton.

Before he reached the front, he understood that if it cost all of them their lives, it would be worth the price. They could never let Forsaken dictate the terms of their existence.

This was more than rescuing their alpha's mate. It was a life and death struggle for what Terry had been fighting for his whole life.

Justice.

"We need to punish them," Merrit whispered when he reached Char.

"I agree whole-heartedly. Help me activate the traps. Rocks. Throw them, hard as you can." Char didn't wait. Between the two of them and Cory, they sent a cascade of gravel into the walls, walking forward a few steps and repeating their efforts. Gene and Aaron stayed close.

Cory looked back when she felt Gene's hot breath on her back.

"Joseph said to spread out," she cried.

"Joseph said that as we get more spread out, the more vulnerable we'll be, if I'm not mistaken," Char answered while continuing to throw gravel.

"Bring it up!" Char yelled and the members of the FDG tightened up, closing in. Mark brought up the rear with two privates, walking backwards to keep their rifles pointed down the tunnel to their rear.

"How far away is he?" Cory asked.

"Not far now, but we have company," Char noted, pulling both pistols and standing ready. She yelled, "HERE THEY COME!"

CHAPTER NINETEEN

NORTH CHICAGO

Timmons and Sue walked out the front door of the mayor's building. "Where did the other pod go?" Timmons asked no one in particular.

"Sorry, sir. Ted climbed in and took off before anyone knew what was going on," Sergeant Boris informed them.

Sue rolled her eyes. "That would be Ted," she stated definitively.

"Is the area secure? All intruders accounted for? What about our own?" Timmons asked.

Boris waved Sergeant Allison over. "We've had a number of civilian casualties. Those assholes fired into any building where they saw people. One of the wolves was shot. Hopefully, she'll live long enough for Cory to return. The wolf has the worst of the injuries. We lost one warrior in the first volley. No one has died after, that I'm aware of, but we have at least ten people shot. I apologize for the number of warriors who dumped their gear and ran," Boris said.

Allison saluted when he arrived. "It looks like we've lost two of the civilians. The others are getting treatment right now from our field medics." Allison looked upset.

The FDG had started to train their people in field medicine. Nearly all of them were capable of working as field medics and some of the more gifted were ready to do more, even surgery if they had to.

Sergeant Allen joined the others in front of the mayor's building. He'd had his people the farthest away from Mayor's Park and had missed most of the action. He had nothing to report from his end.

"Shonna! Would you like to join us for a quick trip to the mountains? I think our alpha needs us," Timmons said, stepping away smartly. Allison's warriors were scattered, as were Allen's, but Boris had his within shouting distance.

"Mount up!" the sergeant yelled, and his people came running. They'd had a taste of the action and wanted more.

They wanted their shot at payback.

❖ ❖ ❖

"I'm going to paint the walls with your blood and then torch this place," Terry taunted as he pushed Yanmei behind him.

"She's going to turn on you, just like she did on me. You see, Terry Henry, there is no one you can trust," the Forsaken countered.

Terry moved back and forth, keeping Kirkus in front of him. Both opponents were tentative. They'd already fought earlier that morning, but back then, Kirkus had a small army with him.

Kirkus had seen what Terry was capable of. But he also

could hear the pain in Terry's mind from his aching muscles.

The Forsaken attacked, angling in toward Terry's injured shoulder, swinging and pounding on that side. Terry blocked blow after blow, but his shoulder wouldn't cooperate for a counter-punch.

Terry lashed out with a forward snap-kick, then a sweep as he tried to knock the Forsaken off balance. To the human observer, the two combatants were only a blur. To Yanmei, their speed was still remarkable, but her enhancements allowed her to keep up.

To Terry, he felt like he was moving slowly.

To Kirkus, he saw openings, but wasn't able to exploit them before they were gone. He reached for Terry's leg during a kick, but the colonel wasn't going to let the Forsaken grab hold. He countered by stopping mid-kick, changing his angle, and driving his foot into Kirkus's face.

The Forsaken was thrown back against the wall.

Terry cornered him, driving a knife hand from his good arm into Kirkus's stomach. The Forsaken gasped as the air exploded from his lungs. Terry followed through, curling his arm and jamming his elbow into Kirkus's throat.

The Forsaken's head bounced off the wall. His knee caught the colonel in the thigh, and an uppercut slipped underneath Terry's raised hands and pounded into his chin.

Terry stumbled backward, covering himself and shaking off the stars. He danced around to make himself a harder target while he gathered his wits.

Kirkus took the respite to drag air into his starved lungs.

The two warriors rested for a moment as they nursed their wounds and glared daggers at each other.

❖ ❖ ❖

Char aimed her pistols, the Glocks that she had taken from Sawyer Browne and carried ever since. She knew rounds were chambered and the weapons were ready to fire. "Stay behind me," Char snapped at Cory.

Gene moved to the side to give himself room. Aaron slipped past Cordelia and stood between her and where he sensed the inbound attackers were coming from. Clovis pranced around and started to bark again. Aaron hissed at the dog, and the big coonhound pup cowered behind his human.

The Forsaken's minions came running, dressed in rags and carrying clubs. Char almost felt bad, but not bad enough that she didn't shoot. One by one, she picked them off, firing a single round at each attacker.

One shot, one kill.

Gene started growling. He was still in pain from the razor storm and wanted to make someone pay.

From the side tunnels, a small number of people popped out. The explosion of gunfire decimated them. It was over in an instant.

The humans had been lackeys. Terry would have called them cannon fodder.

Next were the Forsaken, but they weren't too keen to wade into battle with disciplined troops and Were folk. Merrit headed for the first one that appeared on the flank, but Gene bumped the Werewolf out of the way.

The Werebear bore down on the Forsaken like a freight train. Gene hit the creature and drove him into the wall. He pounded him mercilessly with his massive paws, shredding skin with each strike and then attacking anew. He didn't slow until the Forsaken had been torn to pieces.

But the creature still lived.

"Any more in there?" Mark asked the Werebear. Gene cocked his head as he looked at the captain. Mark continued, "Just watch my back!"

Mark pulled his fighting knife and started removing the creature's head to finish it off once and for all.

The Forsaken that walked into the tunnel in front of Char carried an arrogance common in the stronger of creatures. She holstered her pistols and pulled her knife.

"Sure," the Forsaken said. "I'll start with you. Are you ready for me, bitch?"

The Forsaken knew she was a Werewolf, so she didn't understand if he was trying to be an ass or just noting her status.

"That's alpha bitch to you, dickless," she answered with a smile, crouching and starting to circle her enemy.

He waited, casually. Char wondered what his game was. She didn't sense other Forsaken nearby. She had already walked on the ground between them, so she didn't believe there were any traps.

Could he be that overconfident? she thought, wondering if he heard her.

He smiled, but that disappeared as a large shadow pushed a mass of air toward him.

Gene ran down the Forsaken just like he'd run the previous one down.

This one dodged and didn't bear the full brunt of the charge, but the Werebear stopped instantly when he passed the creature, wheeled, and impaled the Forsaken with one massive set of claws. He lifted the creature with one Werebear arm and slammed him into the wall.

Merrit appeared at Char's side. She stamped a foot and snarled, wanting to carve out her pound of flesh.

"Leave it, my alpha. We all fight for you. Since Gene

seems to have things well in hand, what do you say we go get Terry Henry Walton?"

❖ ❖ ❖

NORTH CHICAGO

Timmons, Sue, Shonna, and as many warriors as could fit climbed into the pod. It took off and pressed them heavily into their seats as it accelerated on an arc that would take it over Chicago, the lake, and back over land where they would start descending toward Mammoth Cave.

"Ted," Timmons said. He and Sue started to chuckle, but sobered quickly. Terry was still missing, and they had no idea how the others were faring inside the cave.

"Are we doing the right thing, Sue?" Timmons asked quietly.

"Going back to the cave?" she wondered, unsure of what he was referring to.

"Being us, being a couple." Timmons looked at the leather boots on his feet. What he wouldn't give for a nice pair of tennis shoes.

Sue put a finger under his chin and lifted his head. "Now listen here. We were meant to be together. Period. End of story. Ted is Ted. No one betrayed anyone else. Are we not friends first?" she asked.

"Yes. We are all friends, much more than just running with the pack," Timmons answered, looking into her beautiful blue eyes. He caressed her blonde hair, tucking a strand behind her ear.

"We could have left, but we didn't, and we won't. We serve our alpha, and in turn, she takes care of us, all of us,"

Sue explained, ending with a big smile. "I couldn't be happier, Timmons. So deal with it, or I'll have to kick your ass upside-down, backwards, and into next week."

"Yes, ma'am!" Timmons grinned as the pod accelerated downward. The screen showed an ETA of five minutes.

Sergeant Boris and his platoon wore grim expressions on their faces. They were ready to go back into battle.

◈ ◈ ◈

TERRY'S PRISON

Terry's nanocytes had been taxed to the limit during his confinement, but the food and water that Yanmei had provided were making the difference. His shoulder was feeling better with each passing moment. The workout had his blood pumping.

The workout. Only Terry Henry Walton would consider hand-to-hand combat to the death to be a workout.

He smiled as he flexed his hands, stretching his fingers until he made loose fists.

"Round two, fuckstick," Terry growled and waded into the fight.

The Forsaken tried a front kick, but Terry was speeding up. He caught Kirkus's leg, twisting and dropping to slam the Forsaken's face into the floor. Terry back-kicked him to the groin, then spun and drove his heel into the side of the creature's head.

Terry let go of Kirkus's leg and jumped on the Forsaken's back, raining a devastating series of strikes to the creature's head.

When blood ran freely from Kirkus's wounds, Terry

picked him up by his legs and spun around, slamming the Forsaken into the wall. TH was enraged, his eyes glowing red. He looked for a weapon, but there wasn't one. Only the chains and Terry's empty shackles.

As Terry dragged the nearly unconscious Forsaken to the prisoner's corner, Yanmei and Fu jumped away. They assumed that Terry was going to chain Kirkus to the wall.

Terry Henry Walton had no intention of leaving the Forsaken alive.

At one point in time, Terry had given Joseph a choice to join the pack or die. Joseph had capitulated. Terry didn't know if he'd ever give another Forsaken such an option. Kirkus had left a bad taste in his mouth.

The colonel wrapped the chain around Kirkus's neck, and Terry pulled and twisted, but the chain's links were too heavy. They crushed the Forsaken's neck skin, but they wouldn't cut through.

He dragged the Forsaken to the doorway and laid the creature with his neck against the doorframe.

Terry slammed the door again and again. He braced the door against the creature's neck and took a running start to kick the door closed with both feet. Kirkus's head came free. Terry exhaled loudly.

The battle was *over*.

Terry ripped the door open and looked into what he had thought was a hallway but was actually a cave tunnel. Sweat ran off his fingers as he offered a hand.

"Come on. We're leaving," Terry told the two women.

CHAPTER TWENTY

Terry looked both ways down the tunnel. He noticed a sign that said Tuberculosis Hospital.

"I'll be damned," Terry said. He saw where the old building had been extended into the cavern. The eyebolts that he was trying to loosen were mounted through two feet of stone, held in place by heavy angle iron.

"I never would have broken those," he mumbled.

He stopped his introspection and listened. The sound of a fighting Werebear was close by, and Terry got the impression that Gene was kicking someone's ass.

"Come on!" he exclaimed, smiling. He knew Char and Cory were near.

Yanmei grabbed him and turned him. He started to put his hands up, but she leaned in and kissed him, gently running one hand down his face.

Clovis scrabbled to a stop and brayed at the Weretiger.

Terry looked up, and when he saw Char, he smiled.

She didn't look happy.

"Hi, lover," he ventured. She crossed her arms and looked at him.

Aaron strolled past, still in Weretiger form. He slapped Clovis with a paw, batting the dog to the side.

"Hey!" Cory yelled through narrowed eyes, unsure of why everyone seemed so tentative.

"Aren't you something," Yanmei said softly, taking a knee so she could look directly into Aaron's Weretiger eyes.

Fu cowered against the wall.

Terry saw the Glock appear in Char's hand.

"Trigger control!" Terry blurted when he saw her finger inside the trigger guard, the same way he'd seen it for decades. She refused to keep her finger off the trigger despite his best training efforts. Char raised the pistol and fired.

"Oops," she said, a smile creeping into the corner of her mouth.

Terry winced and slapped a hand to his side where the bullet had left a tiny crease.

"*That's* trigger control," Char offered, stuffing the pistol back into its holster.

Charumati's eyes sparkled purple and Terry was drawn to them, as he always had been. The rest of the world disappeared as the magic sparkled between the two lovers. They ran into each other's arms.

"For Pete's sake!" Cory exclaimed, her eyes glowing blue. "Did you just shoot my father?"

Char mumbled something into Terry's neck as they hugged fiercely.

"Everyone should know a love like that," Akio whispered.

"Where'd you come from?" Cory asked, shocked at seeing

him next to her and Ayashe next to him.

"Japan," Akio replied simply, before continuing. "I was nursing my wounded dignity, that's all, Cordelia-san."

Gene sniffed and grunted as he joined the group. He stood tall on his back legs.

"Don't you dare, Uncle Gene!" Cory warned, but it was too late. Gene changed into human form, standing naked before the others. The first thing he did was tenderly scratch his chest, crisscrossed with cuts from the razor storm, before reaching around and scratching his butt. Cory stormed up to him and punched him in the arm.

He held his hands out in confusion.

Gene looked around, and once he spotted Fu, the only thing he could think of was that he was naked. He didn't understand why it bothered him, but he only had one choice.

Gene changed back into Werebear form. He slowly approached the woman called Fu, lowering his head so she could scratch his ears, which she did while looking into his big brown eyes.

Two Weretigers stood together before the rooms of the abandoned hospital. No one had seen Yanmei change, but her clothes were neatly stacked on the floor. Fu picked them up and with a hand twisted into Gene's fur, she stayed by his side as they joined Terry and Char.

"Time to go?" Terry asked.

"Captain! Lead us out of here," Char commanded.

"Aye, aye, ma'am!" Mark replied before turning the warriors around. Tail-end Charlie was now on point.

Char and her pack were in the rear. Terry stopped. "My stuff," he said. Yanmei was a Weretiger and no help. Fu was with Gene and she would know, but Aaron, the only one of their group who spoke Chinese, was also in Were form.

"There's nothing you need, because we're not going to go digging around down there," Char told him. "These booby traps were hell. We lost Adams. I thought we'd lost Akio and Joseph, too."

"Adams?" Terry sighed. "Goddamn it! Fucking Forsaken."

"Yeah, fuck those guys," Cory said as she grabbed her father's free arm in both her hands and held on tightly. Clovis ran ahead to bite at the strap hanging from one of the warrior's packs.

"I taught her that," Terry claimed as Char shook her head.

❖ ❖ ❖

The pod hovered over the other three. Timmons and Sue looked for a place to land, but couldn't see anything nearby. They could see Blevins and Heitz sitting in the jeep with their feet propped on the dash. They both looked to be asleep. Or dead.

Blackbeard, Geronimo, and Kiwi stood in the small space between the pods and waved.

Timmons made slow circles until he found a spot nearly a quarter mile away. He set the pod down and the Werewolves led the platoon on a fast run through the woods until they met up with the platoon standing guard duty around the pods.

Ted was in the recovered pod working with the computer interface. Timmons tried to storm in, but Sue stopped him. No one knew Ted better than her.

"Why?" she asked Timmons. He couldn't answer besides wanting to express his dismay at Ted's untimely departure. They knew it would only serve to drive Ted further into a shell.

Sue went into the pod while Timmons tried to find out where Char and the others had gone.

"First time flying the pod, Ted?" Sue asked with a smile.

"Piece of cake," Ted said while continuing to touch the interface screen. Sue rubbed his back like she used to do a long time before. As he did back then, he did not acknowledge her efforts. "Wait for us to come back, Ted, and then we'll all fly out of here. I have a good feeling about this."

Ted mumbled something. Sue wasn't sure if it was meant for her or not. It didn't bother her. She left the pod, walking into Timmons's waiting embrace, and Ted never looked up as he continued to manipulate the pod's touch screen.

"The cave is this way," Timmons said, pointing and striding away. Sue and Shonna fell in behind, as did Boris and the rest of his platoon.

They all noticed that the oldsters were sleeping, but the cover assembly was open on the fifty cal to prevent any discharges. Blackie had told them that Max had lit up Ted's pod. The warriors were both impressed and appalled.

Maybe they were just surprised that Corporal Heitz could hit something. They knew his vision was going.

By the time they reached the cave mouth, Timmons had called a halt. He could feel that the group wasn't far from the entrance and they were casually walking their way.

He felt Char and Terry Henry together.

"They've got him!" Timmons said. He turned to face the platoon and yelled, "They've rescued Terry Henry Walton!"

A cheer went up and continued as Mark and the first two warriors came from the darkness.

Mark smiled and nodded, stepping aside to help people over the last boulder and out of the cave.

They filed out, with Char and Terry Henry coming last.

As usual, the Were folk bore the brunt of the attacks. Even Akio looked in bad shape, which was the first time Timmons had ever seen that.

Joseph had an arm over Merrit's shoulder as the Werewolf helped him. Akio pulled Joseph to the side and handed him a sword that he'd been carrying on his back, forgotten in the turmoil of Terry's capture.

"Damascus steel. You need a sword, Joseph-san," Akio said. The Forsaken took the sword and bowed, unsure of what else to do.

Other members of the Force emerged from the tunnel carrying a body.

Timmons could sense something else was wrong, but he couldn't put his finger on it.

Char stopped when she reached the rest of her pack. "We lost Adams," she said quietly before continuing to walk.

Sue gripped Timmons's arm. "He was never the same after we lost Xandrie," Sue whispered. "I hope he died with honor."

Terry and Char stopped. They turned and walked back to Sue and Timmons. "He died in service to his alpha. He paved our way to my mate, and for that, among a million other things, he will be remembered fondly. Adams was a good Werewolf, an outstanding member of the pack."

Char held her head high as she made sure that Adams was honored for his sacrifice. They would lament his passing later, but for now, this battle was won.

Terry clenched his jaw and nodded to the Force de Guerre as they greeted him warmly, lining both sides of the path to the landing site. Two Weretigers, four Werewolves, and a Werebear followed closely. In the middle of it all, Cordelia walked as both an insider and an outsider, her dog Clovis at her side.

EPILOGUE

"Company, Ah-Ten-Shun!" Terry ordered. The four platoons snapped to the position of attention, frozen in place.

"Warriors to be retired, front and center, march!" Terry commanded.

A small formation in the back of the company ordered a right face, forward march, column left, and proceeded marching until they were standing in front of Colonel Walton.

Captain Mark ordered a hand salute. Blackbeard and Lacy mirrored his motions.

"Ready, two." And they dropped their salutes.

"At ease," Terry ordered loud enough for all to hear.

He was ready to deliver a speech, but couldn't find the words. He waved the group behind him to join him. Jim, James, Gerry, and Kiwi rushed forward.

Ayashe started shaking her head as she watched her parents add to the complete breakdown in discipline. Char joined her husband. They held hands as the groups converged. The platoons remained in formation until their platoon sergeants called them to attention and dismissed them.

Mayra had promised the best feast ever. One steer and two hogs were turning on three different spits. There was even a barbecue sauce made from sugar beets that the older people said rivaled anything from the before time.

Char's pack squeezed in around her. Another one short, leaving them with only six. She knew there were three more in Kentucky and now they had a pod for their own use. She knew what she wanted to do with it. All she had to do was convince TH.

Cory, Marcie, Kae, Kim, Auburn, and the grandchildren watched from the side, talking among themselves as siblings would.

Joseph leaned more deeply into the shadows. It had turned into a very sunny day. He was feeling sated after being allowed to drain the cow's blood before it was slaughtered. He would enjoy the celebration by spending time with his friend, Terry Henry Walton.

But first, there had to be a few words around the fire for those who had died--two privates, Adams, and Billy Spires.

Felicity wore a black armband in honor of her dead husband.

Terry worked his way away from the retirees to stand alone, watching those who had risked all to free him. He still didn't think he had earned that, although he was happy that they'd come. Beneath the surface of his smiling persona, the fire burned.

His eyes glowed red briefly, extinguished through his

force of will. Kirkus didn't know what he unleashed. The war with the Forsaken had only just begun.

THE END

OF

NOMAD AVENGED

Terry Henry Walton will return in Nomad Mortis, June 2017

Don't stop now! Keep turning the pages as both Craig & Michael talk about their thoughts on this book and the overall project called the Terry Henry Walton Chronicles. And artwork! There's a picture of something hiding back there that you *must* see.

NOMAD MORTIS

A SPECIAL LOOK AHEAD

CHAPTER ONE

LOS ANGELES, IN OLD CALIFORNIA, WWDE + 50

"Cut him off! Cut him off!" Char yelled into her communication device.

Lieutenant Boris triggered his device to confirm the order while yelling at the first platoon to haul ass to their secondary location.

Terry Henry Walton slapped Char's butt as he ran past. She took off after him. He had to slow down to let her catch him. Terry became inordinately happy when the guillotine blade was ready to fall on the next Forsaken.

Terry had become obsessed with removing the Forsaken threat from planet earth. He didn't want anyone to go through what he'd gone through, survive what the oldsters in Cheyenne Mountain had survived.

He had declared the Forsaken to be a blight to be wiped out. Terry's moral compass wavered, but he was convinced he was right. He insisted that Joseph be by his side for one final vetting before condemning the Vampires to death.

Akio approved.

Not that last part, just the first bit where the Forsaken as a whole were meant to be wiped out.

Akio and Joseph were not friends. They tolerated each other.

Terry and Char ran like the wind as they gained on the Forsaken. When he emerged from a tunnel, he found himself facing first platoon, lined up to bring the maximum amount of firepower to bear.

Boris barked the order. "Snipers!" And five shots rang out. The Forsaken bounced on his feet from the impact, gasping and wincing as each silver-tipped round slammed through his body.

"Cease fire, we're coming out of the tunnel," Terry yelled into his comm device as he and Char continued to run. Joseph was struggling in the rear. He heard Boris call for the cease-fire.

Terry and Char slowed when they reached the end of the tunnel so Terry could announce their arrival. "Colonel and Major coming out!"

They walked into the open. The Forsaken was still standing, but he had his hands on his knees and gulped for air. They waited at the entrance for Joseph to arrive, before approaching their enemy.

"Good morning," Char said in a light voice.

"I'm not sure it's so good for him," Terry added.

Char shrugged one shoulder.

"Maybe we should tell you, may all your mornings suck worse than this one, but then again, you probably aren't going to have any more mornings, so say your piece. Out with it, so we can get on with the business of killing you," Terry said matter-of-factly, watching for the creature to start squirming.

"Come on, TH, enough with being an asshole. Just kill it," Char grumbled.

Joseph walked past them, approached the Forsaken, and put a hand on his shoulder as if they were old friends.

"He will kill you, you know," Joseph stated. The injured Vampire struggled to stand upright. Joseph helped steady him.

"Why? I wasn't bothering anyone," the creature stuttered.

"Au contraire, asswipe. You've been feeding on humans, and that's a big no-no," Terry answered as he drew his short cavalry blade.

Despite Terry and Char's concerns, Aaron and Yanmei had gone back into Mammoth Cave and recovered Terry's gear. They understood the symbolism of returning Terry in one piece, triumphantly.

They'd done exactly that. When the four pods landed in Mayor's Park, the rescuers and the rescued alike walked out with pride.

Terry couldn't express his appreciation enough to those who risked it all to help him escape. He didn't want to put them in that position again, so to him, the answer was simple.

No Forsaken equaled no unwanted guests kidnapping people.

The logic was irrefutable in Terry's mind.

Joseph stayed between Terry and the other Forsaken. "I'm Joseph. What's your name?"

The Forsaken snarled and growled at Joseph, clamping his jaws shut as a final act of defiance.

"As you wish," Joseph replied and stepped away.

Terry's eyes flashed red while Char's started to glow a soft purple. The Forsaken lunged.

The cavalry blade flashed, and Terry stepped aside to let the headless body stumble and fall to the ground where Terry had been standing.

He looked to Char. She closed her eyes briefly, ventured into the etheric. "All clear." She opened her eyes to look at her husband.

Terry put a hand in the air and twirled it. "Mount up!" he yelled.

Joseph looked at the corpse, mumbled a few words under his breath, and walked away.

Terry cleaned his sword on the Forsaken's clothes and put it back in its scabbard. He took Char's hand in his. "Shall we?" he asked.

"Yes we shall," Char agreed, and without looking at the shriveling body, they turned and headed toward the pod. Terry started to whistle.

"You know that hurts my ears," Char claimed, pointing to the silver streak of hair framing one side of her face.

"I'm sorry," Terry apologized. "Char, I could believe that the dog whistle hurts, but you're as human as I am."

Terry raised an eyebrow as he expected an outburst and a quick wrestling match.

"That cuts me deep, Terry Henry. If I had known that you were prejudice against Werewolves, I would have never spent all these years with you. You shame me, sir!"

Terry smiled, but he was past the friendly banter. He turned serious. "Kirkus fired the first shot. Fuck him and his kind. We'll respond with broadsides until they keep their ugly heads out of sight, and then we'll root them out and watch the sun burn them alive."

"Whatever you feel you have to do," Char replied cautiously. "As long as it doesn't detract from the community. We have people there who are counting on us."

Terry gripped her hand tightly and chewed on the inside of his lip.

"I can't get it out of my head. Getting ripped apart while in chains, getting pummeled. I know it's just pain, but it was the feeling of helplessness." Terry stopped walking and looked down at the ground. His hand hung limply in Char's.

"Helpless? You killed eight of them before they subdued you. Then you killed one more while in captivity, and then you killed Kirkus himself. That doesn't sound helpless to me, TH! And you knew that we'd be coming for you, too," Char told him, purple eyes sparkling as she smiled.

"I know what this is about, TH," Char said softly, frowning. "This is about your self-recrimination from when Melissa was killed. There, you were helpless. She was already dead. The only thing you had left was vengeance. With Kirkus? All you needed to do was buy time. It was completely different this time, my love. You have absolutely nothing to feel bad about."

Char moved in front of him and straightened his eyebrows with one index finger, drawing it slowly over his eyes. "You've got a couple crazy hairs going on here. I'll need to clip those when we get back."

Terry wanted to laugh, but Melissa was on his mind. It had been forever since that time. He knew that he'd been forgiven because he forgave himself. Kirkus was still in his head, but he comforted himself by thinking of how he ripped the creature's head off.

"One of your cleaner cuts, TH. I like the improved technique," Char said as she trailed a finger down his face to gently caress his lips.

"I want a clean kill. Even the Forsaken shouldn't have to suffer," Terry replied as his blue eyes grew ice cold. "I guess I became judge and jury, too, and their sentence is a foregone conclusion. Their crime is their very existence, and I'm going to fucking kill them all."

❖ ❖ ❖

Felicity sat in the mayor's office looking at the chalkboard with the columns and the numbers. Sue was there and had just updated the board after hearing the latest reports.

"What are those Weathers' boys doing out there?" she asked.

The cattle herd was growing faster than the demands for meat.

"We need more people, or the Weathers clan is going to have to keep those bulls penned up," Sue replied before pointing to a different column. "Fishing fleet is maintaining status quo."

Felicity mumbled her agreement.

"I could use some sun. Join me?" Felicity got up from her desk and headed for the door. She didn't have to ask Sue twice.

When they made it outside, Sue already had her shirt tied up, exposing her mid-section.

They found a spot on the grass and laid down.

"Tell me about Ted," Felicity asked out of the blue.

"What?" Sue asked, rolling on her side to see if Felicity was joking.

Felicity played with the blades of grass. "I don't want to outlive another man," she whispered, looking ashamed for saying the words out loud.

Sue had not worried about that aspect since she only had two partners and they were both Werewolves. Normal humans never held any appeal as they were too fragile.

"Ted has one of the kindest souls you'll ever meet, but he

can be so infuriating. He doesn't even know you exist ninety-nine percent of the time. That's probably the worst of it. All you have to do is be inside the small window through which he is looking at that moment, and it's good. Otherwise, you might as well be alone," Sue advised.

"I already am alone, and I have been for some time already," Felicity confided.

The wolf pack ran into Mayor's Park followed closely by a braying coonhound pup. Cory was with them. Felicity had hoped Ted would be with them. Sue was glad that he was not.

❖ ❖ ❖

The pod landed in the new landing zone, the LZ, on what used to be the naval station's athletic fields. They'd become heavily overgrown over the past fifty years, but the warriors weren't deterred. They'd hacked the growth away, and then lit a fire to burn the rest. The fire burned out of control briefly, but after a short period of panic and flailing, they stopped it from spreading.

The buildings beside the LZ were being recovered and rebuilt into a proper barracks to house the entirety of the Force de Guerre. The motor pool was on the other side along with the lake. That gave the FDG the most options for a quick response.

Especially since they had their own pod.

They wanted to build a hangar for it but were at a loss as to how to do that without heavy equipment. They had the steam engine and the train, but that wasn't a crane or a bulldozer.

Ted looked at it as he walked past on his morning stroll to the power plant. He heard what the others were saying, but none of it made sense.

None of them were engineers, and they had yet to ask for engineering help. Ted couldn't understand why.

"Just use the pod," he said, shaking his head as he walked away.

Lieutenant Boris, Sergeant Allison and the newly promoted Corporal Ayashe looked at each other. They seemed to be happiest arguing about how to build the hangar. Once they had their answer, they felt stupid.

"Son of a bitch," Allison whined before the others burst out laughing.

"Fucking engineers," Boris added, but he knew Ted was right. "Let's ask Timmons and Shonna when they come by, then we'll go find what we need, stage it here, and get someone who can fly that thing to help us put this together. We'll have to get clearance from the colonel. He looks at this thing like it's his baby."

Ayashe nodded knowingly. Because of her parents, she'd spent a great deal of time growing up with Terry, Char, and their children. Kim and Kae had been her babysitters too many times to count. Ayashe understood how the colonel felt about having his own transportation.

Being mobile had always been a goal of his, from horses to wheeled vehicles, to sailboats, to the pods.

They'd used the pod one time so far and the results, in Terry's mind, were spectacular. He called his new strategy "search and destroy." With Akio's help, they located and mapped groups of people where Forsaken might be present. Then they would fly over an area late at night and let Joseph and the Were folk do their thing.

When they pinpointed a Forsaken, they did a quick reconnaissance using FDG assets that wouldn't necessarily alert the Forsaken, and then they swooped in. The tac team made up exclusively of Weres surrounded the Forsaken. They had cornered it, and Terry had finished it off.

Ayashe wanted her chance but knew that she needed to train more, get stronger and faster. "When's training?" she asked. Boris and Allison looked at her oddly.

"Maybe we'll cancel it while we're figuring out what we need for the hangar," the new lieutenant replied.

The corporal was shocked. "We never cancel training!" she exclaimed. "Let me run it while you guys get into a circle jerk."

"At ease, Corporal!" Allison ordered, frowning at the insubordination.

Boris started to laugh. "I guess you're right. Leave it to us grunts to take all day doing something the engineers can do while they're eating lunch. And we wouldn't do it half as well. Allison, run the training. Five-mile run, followed by hand-to-hand combat training. Black-belt-level. "

"Aye, aye, Sergeant!" Ayashe replied and ran for the new barracks where she'd stashed her training gear.

AUTHOR'S NOTES - CRAIG MARTELLE

Written: May 17, 2017

Thank you for reading to this point. That is incredible – book 7 in the series and you're still reading. You make this journey of ours worthwhile.

Nomad Avenged was shaped because of reader input. With the break between books 6 and 7, a number of you reached out to me, telling me what you liked and what you didn't like. That was all great stuff! I have taken your input into account, so in essence, this book is written to answer your questions in a way that I hope makes sense.

Char is the alpha, make no mistake about that. Terry is a fierce warrior, even in captivity. He isn't afraid of anything, the least of which are Forsaken, although they are formidable. Terry loves the challenge, both mental and physical when dealing with the creatures.

He's always happy to see people he trained fight the Forsaken, dominating them, and showing that the big baddies may not be so bad, as long as you've honed your body into a weapon.

This book jumps twenty-five years into the future. Unfortunately, we don't see a few of the characters from the previous books. Those folks, like Kiwi and Lacy need their own stories, short stories telling their tale. That's something that I will do, every week, on Wednesday, publishing a new short story about a character within the Terry Henry Walton Chronicles. I will do this – put out short stories and compile them into a novella that we'll make available on Amazon when we have enough words.

Most importantly, out of everything going on – my tractor is fixed! The ground v-belt idler wheel seized and that's why it had issues. It took me calling on my neighbor for help. He is a certified mechanic, but the real trick was that it took two of us. I had to stand on the brakes which moved the armature into a position where he could get a socket and a 14" ratchet on it. Cracking it free was easy after that. I swapped out the wheel, hit it with some oil, and re-tightened everything. The tractor started right up and I drove it out of the garage and to the shed – drove like a champ. I even fired up the snowblower to make sure that baby would spin without making a sound and it did, very nicely.

We also had our driveway fixed. Great Northwest dumped two truckloads of RAP (recycled asphalt product) into a huge dip that had developed over the last five years. They watered it in, mashed it down in even layers and now our driveway is an easy climb. My tractor will appreciate it come winter. I got stuck quite a few times trying to climb that sharp rise after a big dip.

In between, I have a garden to start! The greenhouse is up and ready to receive its first little starter plants, which we buy. I don't start them in the garage. No need. All kinds of folks show up at the first couple Farmer's Markets with seedlings. Getting things going right now is important because our growing season is so short. 75-day tomatoes are right on the edge of not making it, like last year when they didn't ripen before our first frost.

I also need to prepare the garden dirt with more manure and other plant goodies. I'll dig down two feet for the tomato plants and put a bunch of stuff in the bottom of the hole – fish, aspiring, egg shells, and a couple other things. I found a website with the best information.

http://realfarmacy.com/correctly-plant-tomatoes-get-5-8ft-plants/

I have high hopes for my tomatoes this year. Really high hopes because it can't be as bad as last year.

At least the rhubarb came back and stronger than ever. I planted the first one as a test last year and seeing it come back means that I got it right. We'll plant two more this year and that'll be it. Three years before they are ready to harvest after replanting, but we have time.

Phyllis, our nearly 10-year-old pit bull is doing well! A year ago she had ACL surgery and that was all documented on Animal Planet. Phyllis is a TV star! I got some air time, too, but this isn't about me. It's Phyllis's turn. She is back up to nearly full speed, but has slowed down. She loves being outside this time of year, although at 60 degrees Fahrenheit, it is a little warm for her. She pants like she's in a sauna.

She is acclimated to where we live. We'll see a few days in the 80s, but generally, summer highs only reach into the 70s.

Two days ago, we started our annual run of 72 days straight with twenty-four hours of daylight. Yes, it's light all the time. I get up way early so taking Phyllis for her walk at 3 am. I wore shorts and a sweatshirt this morning. It was 40 outside. Just like summer!

What the hell is next? How about Nomad Mortis! Terry goes to war against the Forsaken, those bastards. How did they think taking him prisoner was a good idea?

They called down the thunder.

I have a couple anthologies that I'm editing and publishing in June. One is an epic military/space opera/space adventure science fiction collection with twenty-three authors ranging from NY Times Bestselling, to USA Today bestsellers to multiple Amazon bestseller. This really is an epic collection and all stories are exclusive to The Expanding Universe, Volume 2 to be published on June 15th. It is available for pre-order now.

https://www.amazon.com/dp/B072LMWBWT

The second anthology is because I'm a role-playing gamer from back in the 70s. I've had the pleasure to reconnect with James M. Ward, who wrote Deities and Demigods for AD&D, along with a vast number of modules and books. He's also the creator of the first science fiction role-playing game, Metamorphosis Alpha, followed by Gamma World. We have ten authors with ten short stories based on the starship Warden. That volume should go to our formatter in just a couple days so we can publish the paperback and the eBook at the same time. Look for Metamorphosis Alpha – Chronicles from the Warden, coming in June, 2017.

With that, I'm back to it, lots to do.

❖ ❖ ❖

Please join my Newsletter, or you can follow me on Facebook since you'll get the same opportunity to pick up the books on that first day they are published.

If you liked this story, you might like some of my other books. You can join my mailing list by dropping by my website **www.craigmartelle.com** or if you have any comments, shoot me a note at craig@craigmartelle.com. I am always happy to hear from people who've read my work. I try to answer every email I receive.

If you liked the story, please write a short review for me

on Amazon. I greatly appreciate any kind words, even one or two sentences go a long way. The number of reviews an ebook receives greatly improves how well an ebook does on Amazon.

Amazon – www.amazon.com/author/craigmartelle
Facebook – www.facebook.com/authorcraigmartelle
My web page – www.craigmartelle.com
Twitter – www.twitter.com/rick_banik

Thank you for reading Terry Henry Walton Chronicles!

AUTHOR'S NOTES - MICHAEL ANDERLE

Written: May 30, 2017

First, THANK YOU for not only reading this book, but making it to my author notes after Awesome Craig's, as well!

Now, I have absolutely zero stories about growing tomatoes. My father could tell me his stories, and I could type them up, but I have no personal tomato stories to tell. My version of a good tomato is one that has been liquified and stuck in a bottle.

I suppose I could tell you about my massive issues deciding what kind of ketchup to purchase when an off-brand is selling for cheap in the store. Then I figure out if the off-brand company screwed with the basic ketchup recipe or not.

However, I *doubt* that is a riveting conversation.

When I wrote Death Becomes Her which is the book that started the whole Kurtherian Gambit Universe that we all write in now, it was in part because it was a bucket list item.

You know, "Write a Book!" kind of bucket list item?

The slightly bigger part of the kick in my pants to make it happen, however, was a little more primitive. It was a father's need to help one of his children. Parenting, if you are a parent, but no kids are out of the house yet, doesn't stop at eighteen. Dammit.

I have to admit that wasn't what I believed as the first of three sons were growing up. I thought "Eighteen and they go off into the world" which (if my memory serves me mostly intact) was what I thought I had accomplished as a kid.

I believe my father might, just might, have a slightly different tale.

So, the second part of my starting to write was 'I need to do this to be able to explain, with confidence, to my oldest son' sort of thing (D'artagnan Anderle - Pen'ish name). His personality is a bit different than mine, and he is a whole lot younger than I am (25 years or so younger). I figured that I could write a few books, work out the kinks, and then let him know the parts he was missing and off he would go.

That *really* didn't work. I was (perhaps) wanting his success for different reasons than he might want the success.

In fact, being brutally honest now, I know it.

When I first encouraged him to write a book, it was a no go.

It was "*not something he wanted to do.*"

That was a let down for me. I've shared this part of the story in previous author notes. I had to come to terms with the full circle of life not happening and that he just didn't want to write, whether he had the talent or not.

Then, we spoke again a couple of months later on the subject.

During this conversation, we discussed it wasn't that he didn't want to write, but rather he didn't know *what* to write about. A definitive story that was him. (For those who don't know, neither D'artagnan nor Joey write like I write. Their personal voice isn't the same and often my suggestions get either one of them to look at me like sons and daughters have looked at parents for millenia... "are you kidding me, Dad?")

So, D'artagnan gave me two different story beginnings and I provided feedback. Fast forward four months as he worked, deleted, wrote, erased all to figure *himself* out as much as any early author has to in life. Meaning, *who am I as a creator? What makes me tick, something I'm interested in writing about?*

A couple of months ago, the Author's Wife (AKA Mom) and I went down to see him in the Houston area. He and I hung out for an afternoon and discussed the story ideas which he had been working on.

We discussed how he had started down the path of writing those other stories, how he had crashed and burned, and what it took for him to really bring out of himself the plot, the characters and the malefics that kept his imagination working in overdrive. Further, we discussed the specifics of how writing a book works, what it takes to get it edited, covers, and a whole lot more.

By then, I had learned that I *couldn't* push authors. If he was going to do this, it had to be on his own.

This knowledge had not come from working with D'artagnan, but from the many other authors I had counseled over the last year which I put into practice mentoring my oldest son.

As a father, I wanted so desperately to see him succeed. As a publisher, I needed him to understand how it all works. The good, and the bad.

The "stuff that is fun, and the stuff that is dressed in coveralls and looks a lot like *work*."

He got off to an amazing start. Knocked out 15,000 words pretty quickly.

Then stalled.

I had to gently ask what is going on, not ping him (easy to do in Slack, where all of my work gets done with other authors, editors and artists.) Then, we might not chat for a few days as he did stuff. What stuff? I've no clue - I didn't ask.

I had to be patient. Let him get through the hard stuff, work it all out in his own internal way.

Basically, it kinda sucked to be honest. As a parent, I just wanted the amazing to happen and off to the next awesome milestone in his life he would go.

However, I grew as well. I grew a little as I allowed him to work it out. I grew to know that each time he would come back, that he hadn't dropped the project (probably one of my biggest fears, honestly) and that what he came back with… was stronger.

D'artagnan worked with Jen McDonnell and then Lynne Stiegler on the editing side. He worked with Jeff Brown on the covers.

He, like Joey before him, has his own damned opinions and apparently, they aren't so afraid of best selling author Michael Anderle to tell him 'No, they didn't like what he was suggesting!'

In fact, you could say they didn't really *CARE* about whatever accolades and accomplishments their dad had built up, I was *still* just dad. Oh, they respected my accomplishments, but they aren't overwhelmed by what I've accomplished to do what I say without questioning it. They, annoyingly enough…

Have their own opinion on their work.

Whether it is with Joey and "killing off some characters" or D'artagnan and his "the covers look better this way" they both will take stands on their work, and it doesn't matter what my accomplishements and opinions are, this is how their art is going to be.

And I'm DAMNED proud of them standing on their own two feet as they build their own career.

Each one is different, each one is uniquely themselves.

Each one, I believe, has something to offer readers. Some of my readers will like their stuff, others won't and *that's ok.*

With D'artagnan, he enjoys a story where everything isn't so black and white. Where, as the intro blurb to his book talks about, the Chosen might not want to save the world because it is the right thing to do.

He might want to do it because he wants *revenge.*

Not everything in life is black and white and the path to

getting to the end might be a challenge.

That is D'Artagnan's voice more than mine. The ability to weave a story where you might get to the same ending, but the path is …

Frankly, not the way I would write it.

So, if you would like to read a brand new author, an author that needed to know more about the Indie Publishing area before he was willing to stick his own toes into the water, I'd like to be the first to introduce you to…

D'artagnan Anderle - The Author of Sevanouir: Rebirth
(The Strange Tales of the Malefic - Book 01)
(Link is Below.)

What if the chosen want revenge over destiny?

Sylas Chevalier is the latest son of a lineage of Maleficus, users of powerful and mystical items known as Malefics, to inherit his family's blade, Sevanouir.

However, it came at a terrible cost.

Now a part of a reality that he once thought was a joke, Sylas gets a crash course in the world of his forebearers and must learn what it means to be the wielder of this blade, as mysterious forces approach with their own desires and intent, and they need Sylas and his blade for themselves.

Willingly or not.

❖ ❖ ❖

Check out more on Amazon using the amazing 'go to the right country' link:
http://books2read.com/Sevanouir-Rebirth

THE TERRY HENRY WALTON CHRONICLES

THE KUTHERIAN GAMBIT SERIES

FREE TRADER SERIES

CYGNUS SPACE OPERA - SET IN THE FREE TRADER UNIVERSE

END TIMES ALASKA SERIES,
A WINLOCK PRESS PUBLICATION

Book 1: Endure
Book 2: Run
Book 3: Return
Book 4: Fury

RICK BANIK THRILLERS

People Raged and the Sky Was on Fire
The Heart Raged (2017)
Paranoid in Paradise (Short Story - 2017)

SHORT STORY CONTRIBUTIONS TO ANTHOLOGIES

Earth Prime Anthology, Volume 1
(Stephen Lee & James M. Ward)
Apocalyptic Space Short Story Collection
(Stephen Lee & James M. Ward)
Lunar Resorts Anthology, Volume 2
(Stephen Lee & James M. Ward)
Just One More Fight
(published as a novella standalone)
The Expanding Universe, Volume 1
(edited by Craig Martelle)
The Expanding Universe, Volume 2
(edited by Craig Martelle – June 2017)
The Misadventures of Jacob Wild McKilljoy
(with Michael-Scott Earle)
Metamorphosis Alpha, Stories from the Starship
Warden
(with James M. Ward – Summer 2017)

MICHAEL ANDERLE
KUTHERIAN GAMBIT SERIES TITLES INCLUDE:

FIRST ARC
Death Becomes Her (01) - Queen Bitch (02) - Love Lost (03) - Bite This (04) - Never Forsaken (05) - Under My Heel (06) - Kneel Or Die (07)

SECOND ARC
We Will Build (08) - It's Hell To Choose (09) - Release The Dogs of War (10) - Sued For Peace (11) - We Have Contact (12) - My Ride is a Bitch (13) - Don't Cross This Line (14)

THIRD ARC *(Due 2017)*
Never Submit (15) - Never Surrender (16) - Forever Defend (17) - Might Makes Right (18) - Ahead Full (19) - Capture Death (20) - Life Goes On (21)

New Kutherian Gambit Series
THE SECOND DARK AGES
The Dark Messiah
The Darkest Night *(Soon)*
Darkest Before the Dawn *(07.2017)*
Light Is Breaking *(11.2017)*

THE BORIS CHRONICLES
With Paul C. Middleton

Evacuation
Retaliation
Revelation
Restitution *(2017)*

RECLAIMING HONOR
With Justin Sloan

Justice Is Calling (01)
Claimed By Honor (02)
Judgment Is Coming (03)
Angel of Reckoning (04) (*Soon*)

THE ETHERIC ACADEMY
With TS Paul

ALPHA CLASS (01)
ALPHA CLASS (02)
ALPHA CLASS (03) (*Early Summer 2017*)

TERRY HENRY "TH" WALTON CHRONICLES
With Craig Martelle

Book 1 – Nomad Found
Book 2 – Nomad Redeemed
Book 3 - Nomad Unleashed
Book 4 - Nomad Supreme
Book 5 – Nomad's Fury
Book 6 – Nomad Justice
Book 7 – Nomad Avenged
Book 8 – Nomad Mortis
Book 9 – Nomad's Force
Book 10 – Nomad's Galaxy

TRIALS AND TRIBULATIONS
With Natalie Grey

Book 1 – Risk Be Damned
Book 2 – Damned to Hell
Book 3 - Hell's Worst Nightmare

THE ASCENSION MYTH
With Ell Leigh Clarke

Book 1 – Awakened
Book 2 – Activated

THE RISE OF MAGIC
With CM Raymond / LE Barbant

Book 1 – Restrictions
Book 2 – Reawakening
Book 3 – Rebellion
Book 4 – Revolution (coming soon)

THE HIDDEN MAGIC CHRONICLES
With Justin Sloan

Book 1 – Shades of Light

SHORT STORIES
Frank Kurns Stories of the Unknownworld 01 (*7.5*)
You Don't Mess with John's Cousin
Frank Kurns Stories of the Unknownworld 02 (*9.5*)
Bitch's Night Out
Frank Kurns Stories of the Unknownworld 03 (13.25)
BELLATRIX
With Natalie Grey

AUDIOBOOKS
Available at Audible.com and iTunes

THE KURTHERIAN GAMBIT
Death Becomes Her - Available Now
Queen Bitch – Available Now
Love Lost – Available Now
Bite This - Available Now

Never Forsaken - Available Now
Under My Heel - Available Now

RECLAIMING HONOR SERIES
Justice Is Calling – Available Now
Claimed By Honor – Available Now
Judgement Has Fallen - Available Now
Angel of Reckoning - Coming Soon

TERRY HENRY "TH" WALTON CHRONICLES
Nomad Found
Nomad Redeemed
Nomad Unleashed - Available Soon

THE ETHERIC ACADEMY
Alpha Class
Alpha Class 2

ANTHOLOGIES
Glimpse
Honor in Death
(Michael's First Few Days)

Beyond the Stars: At Galaxy's Edge
Tabitha's Vacation

CRAIG MARTELLE SOCIAL

For a chance to see ALL of Craig's new Book Series
Check out his website below!

Website:
http://www.craigmartelle.com

Email List:
http://www.craigmartelle.com
(Go 1/2 way down his first page, the box is in the center!)

Facebook Here:
https://www.facebook.com/AuthorCraigMartelle/

MICHAEL ANDERLE SOCIAL

Website:
http://kurtherianbooks.com/

Email List:
http://kurtherianbooks.com/email-list/

Facebook Here:
https://www.facebook.com/TheKurtherianGambitBooks/

Made in the USA
Las Vegas, NV
22 June 2024

91336543R10136